# SOMETHING FROM MERCURY

# Borgo Press Books by JOHN RUSSELL FEARN

*1,000-Year Voyage: A Science Fiction Novel*
*Black Maria, M.A.: A Classic Crime Novel*
*The Crimson Rambler: A Crime Novel*
*Don't Touch Me: A Crime Novel*
*Dynasty of the Small: Classic Science Fiction Stories*
*The Empty Coffins: A Mystery of Horror*
*The Fourth Door: A Mystery Novel*
*From Afar: A Science Fiction Mystery*
*The G-Bomb: A Science Fiction Novel*
*Here and Now: A Science Fiction Novel*
*Into the Unknown: A Science Fiction Tale*
*Last Conflict: Classic Science Fiction Stories*
*The Man from Hell: Classic Science Fiction Stories*
*The Man Who Was Not: A Crime Novel*
*One Way Out: A Crime Novel* (with Philip Harbottle)
*Pattern of Murder: A Classic Crime Novel*
*Reflected Glory: A Dr. Castle Classic Crime Novel*
*Robbery Without Violence: Two Science Fiction Crime Stories*
*Rule of the Brains: Classic Science Fiction Stories*
*Shattering Glass: A Crime Novel*
*The Silvered Cage: A Scientific Murder Mystery*
*Slaves of Ijax: A Science Fiction Novel*
*Something from Mercury: Classic Science Fiction Stories*
*The Space Warp: A Science Fiction Novel*
*The Time Trap: A Science Fiction Novel*
*Vision Sinister: A Scientific Detective Thriller*
*What Happened to Hammond? A Scientific Mystery*
*Within That Room!: A Classic Crime Novel*

# SOMETHING FROM MERCURY

## CLASSIC SCIENCE FICTION STORIES

### JOHN RUSSELL FEARN

THE BORGO PRESS
MMXII

SOMETHING FROM MERCURY

Copyright © 1939, 1941 1946, 1954 by John Russell Fearn
Copyright © 2012 by Philip Harbottle

FIRST BORGO PRESS EDITION

Published by Wildside Press LLC

www.wildsidebooks.com

# DEDICATION

*For Arthur King*

# CONTENTS

ACKNOWLEDGMENTS . . . . . . . . . . . . . . .9
SOMETHING FROM MERCURY . . . . . . . . . 11
THE WORLD THAT DISSOLVED . . . . . . . . 51
PRE-NATAL . . . . . . . . . . . . . . . . . . . . . 73
BEYOND ZERO . . . . . . . . . . . . . . . . . . . 91
ACROSS THE AGES . . . . . . . . . . . . . . . 133
TWILIGHT PLANET . . . . . . . . . . . . . . . 151
ABOUT THE AUTHOR . . . . . . . . . . . . . . 175

# ACKNOWLEDGMENTS

These stories were previously published as follows, and are reprinted by permission of the author's estate and his agent, Cosmos Literary Agency:

"Something from Mercury" was first published in *The British Science Fiction Magazine*, #6, 1954. Copyright © 1954 by John Russell Fearn; Copyright © 2012 by Philip Harbottle.

"The World That Dissolved" was first published in *Amazing Stories,* February 1939. Copyright © 1939 by John Russell Fearn; Copyright © 2012 by Philip Harbottle.

"Pre-Natal" was first published in *Outlands* #1, 1946. Copyright © 1946 by John Russell Fearn; Copyright © 1973 by Carrie Fearn; Copyright © 2012 by Philip Harbottle.

"Beyond Zero" was first published in *Vargo Statten Science Fiction Magazine* #1, 1954. Copyright © 1954 by John Russell Fearn; Copyright © 2012 by Philip Harbottle.

"Across the Ages" was first published in *Future Combined with Science Fiction,* October 1941. Copyright © 1941 by John Russell Fearn; Copyright ©

2012 by Philip Harbottle.

"Twilight Planet" was first publishing in *Thrilling Wonder Stories*, Fall 1946. Copyright © 1946 by John Russell Fearn; Copyright © 2012 by Philip Harbottle.

# SOMETHING FROM MERCURY

It came originally from the merciless, frost-bound wilderness of the night side of Mercury, that hemisphere temporarily turned from the raging cauldron of the sun—Mercury, a slowly rotating, tortured world, which for uncounted generations has alternated between blazing solar heat and a long night facing the frigid stars, its surface split by the extremes of temperature into deep ravines.

Harry Dagenham brought it back to Earth—which was just about the crazy sort of thing Harry would do. Never a thought of consequences; never a thought of anything except that he had discovered a petrified snake—or something—on Mercury's night side and wanted the Earthly recordists to have it.

Certainly the thing looked like a snake. I remember that, on his second night back on Earth, Harry Dagenham brought the object with him in a specimen box. He wanted our select little circle to see it—a kind of preview before he handed the thing on to the Interplanetary Authorities on the following day—and so there started for us a night of unbridled terror.

You can picture our little reunion scene very easily. Dinner was over and we were assembled in the big, comfortable lounge of Giles Ascroft's home. Some of you may remember Giles Ascroft as one of the first men to travel to Mars way back in 2087. He is an old man now, but still vigorous. Nothing could be more fitting, though, than that he should throw a celebration party for Harry Dagenham, leader of the intrepid little expedition who had just safely completed the first journey to Mercury—the hell-planet, a world more difficult to reach than any other because of the sun's terrifying nearness and the stupendous gravitational warps existing within the Mercutian orbit.

So, then, there were Giles Ascroft, silver-haired and a vigorous talker; Trudy, his fast-ageing but gracious wife; Harry Dagenham himself, short, wiry, red-haired, with a sawn-off nose; Lucy Clinton, my fiancée—and lastly myself, Duncan Fields. Four of us listening to Harry's endlessly energetic narrative of his experiences on the hell-world.

"The fact remains, the job's done!" he kept reiterating, as though to convince himself that he really had come back from that awful region so close beside Old Sol. "Except for the photographs, movie reels, rock samples, and recorded effects we brought back with us, I could almost think we dreamed the whole thing. You can all of you judge that I'm not exactly the nervous type, but *Mercury*...." He gave a little shiver, then held a beefy hand aloft. "May I never have to visit that planet again."

"You never will," I told him, smiling. "As one of the Interplanetary Executive, I know their plans for a good way ahead, and there's no mention of ever asking the same crew to again make the Mercutian trip. Others, maybe—but not you or your boys."

"Oh, maybe they wouldn't mind." There was a faraway look in Harry's daredevil eyes. "But I had enough—quite enough. I can remember how that night plain looked when I wandered across it. Despite the nearness of the spaceship, there was about me an awful, indescribable loneliness. To the left lay low mountain ranges and over the top of them were the writhing tips of the solar prominences. That was the only sign of what one could call real life. Otherwise there were the glacial stars, the grey and frost-broken plateau, and the everlasting airless desolation."

"Why did you bother to go onto the night plain anyway?" Lucy asked in surprise—for, not being particularly interested in interplanetary matters, she had no conception of how a space traveller feels when he reaches another world.

"Why?" Harry stared at her. "*Why?* Because I had to! One just couldn't be content to *look* at the night plateau and not do something about it. I had to get the feel of Mercury. So I slipped on my spacesuit and sallied forth.... Glad I did, too. I found remains of life, which shows that at some time Mercury must have had a form of life upon it, even if it was snakelike."

That, then, was how the business started. It suddenly dawned upon Harry in the midst of his narrative that he had brought his Mercutian specimen with him for all of us to see. And, excusing himself, he left the lounge and hurried outside to his car.

Old Giles Ascroft shook his head slowly, and then gazed out onto the mellow calm of the summer night.

"Not altogether sure that I like it," he commented.

"Like what, dear?" His wife looked surprised. "It seems to be more or less settled weather to me. Once a calm spell sets in we—"

"I'm talking about specimens." Ascroft said. "I remember that when I was a young space explorer, I brought back some seeds and they were planted in the Botanical Gardens. What a rumpus there was! The infernal things proved to be carnivorous and, in full bloom, attacked animals and human beings alike. Specimens from other worlds can be damned dangerous sometimes."

"I cannot see," Lucy said thoughtfully, her dark eyes pensive, "that anything particularly lethal can come from Mercury. Anyway, it's dead—or so Harry said. So why worry about it?"

Ascroft shrugged. "Not worrying, m'dear, just remarking."

At this moment Harry came back into the lounge, the battered specimen-box in his brawny hand. He snatched up the evening paper, laid it on the polished table, then set the box down upon it. After which, with a needless amount of dramatic flourishing, he unclamped the lid and raised it.

"What this is I'll be damned if I know," he confessed

frankly. "You see it now just as I saw it on the Night Side. Tell me what you think about it, Mr. Ascroft. You're a specialist on alien life forms. That's why I've brought it to you before handing it over to the Interplanetary Executive."

Ascroft shivered, getting up and crossing to the table. "Mercury is an unknown world. 'Fraid I shan't be much help here."

Harry shrugged and lifted his specimen from the box, holding it up so we could all see it. I felt I wanted to laugh—and in fact Lucy did. A kind of half nervous giggle.

"Cotton reels!" she exclaimed, as convulsed as a schoolgirl. "Just like cotton reels!"

She was surprisingly right. Being a gossip columnist by profession, her mind always worked in similes—so I'll leave her description as the best one. The Mercutian specimen did look like a dozen small cotton reels all strung together. What made the object all the more fantastic was the fact that it did not bend in the least, even though Harry was holding it upwards in the air by the tail. The effect was odd—those dozen reels bending like a warm candle, yet remaining rigid.

"So that's it!" Giles Ascroft stared at it. "Nothing very remarkable about it—"

"Only on closer examination, sir," Harry corrected him. "You can see a head, and a tail. See...."

He laid the specimen on the newspaper beside the specimen box, and we all crowded round for a closer look. Since the table light was switched on, its diagonal brilliance etched the specimen out clearly, and now it became obvious that the 'reels' were held together by some wiry kind of tissue, which looked as though it were petrified into stone. For that matter, the entire object was dull grey in colour, and looked like the end of a rattlesnake's tail.

This, though, was the whole specimen. It had a tapering point which marked the tail extremity, whilst the head end was as thin as a spade except for bony ridges jutting over tightly closed eyes. There was a mouth, too, or rather a trap. At the moment it seemed like a thin scar travelling the length of the spade-shaped head. I imagined that if that mouth opened, it would split the head in half.

"Of all the horrible, vicious-looking things!" Lucy declared at last. "All I can say is, thank heaven it's dead!"

"Dead as the fictional doornail," Harry agreed, "I wouldn't have been reckless enough to bring a live specimen here!" He lifted up the specimen and let it drop again with a brittle bang. "And as tough as anything I've ever struck. Just watch this!"

Taking the specimen by head and tail he placed it across his thigh and then shoved with all his great strength. The specimen remained rigid and unbending, hard as iron itself.

"I've tried smashing it over a piece of teak," Harry said. "All I got was a badly wrenched arm and a slight scar on the teak."

"But why try and smash it?" Lucy demanded. "That

would ruin it as a specimen."

"Yes, I suppose it would, but somehow I've been wanting to satisfy myself why any form of life—or rather death—can be so hard. It just doesn't make sense. Even the hardest of our known substances is capable of being smashed by something or other."

"So far as this specimen goes," Ascroft remarked dryly, "I don't doubt that a trip-hammer would be able to take care of it. However, joking apart, it's an interesting sidelight on Mercutian life—if that is what it once was."

"How can it be anything else?" Harry demanded.

"I don't know—but there is always the possibility that you were not the first man to reach Mercury. Others from outer space might have got there before you and left this behind. It might have been something savage which was best to get rid of. So it was thrown outside and after that the airless hell of Mercury took care of it.... However, all this is pure conjecture. What we need to do is have a closer look at the thing in the laboratory. Its structure is definitely unique. Bring it along, Harry, will you?"

Ascroft had been leading the way to the lounge door whilst speaking, and now we all trooped after him, including Lucy.

Though she had already openly expressed her dislike of the specimen, it was evidently not violent enough to prevent her being interested in further developments concerning it.

Ascroft had quite a comprehensive laboratory

attached to his home, but when all of us were within it, there was precious little room. However, we crowded in and then stood near the bench as Ascroft switched on the powerful shadowless floodlights, and then set the electron microscope in operation. We would have made quite a picture as we stood there, watching, our forms silhouetted against the blaze of light concentrated on the subject, and Ascroft's tall form bending to the lenses of the microscope. When at length he straightened up, his expression was one of considerable mystification.

"This certainly doesn't enter into the category of any form of life I ever heard of," he commented. "From the look of it, it might just as well be rock itself. And that cartilage of tissue stuff between the 'cotton reels' is composed of multi-millions of fibres, just like meshed wires! Y'know something, Harry?"

"What, sir?"

"I'm beginning to wonder if this isn't perhaps a model of some kind—something left behind by a Mercutian civilisation—just as we have models of prehistoric animals in our museums."

"Could be, I suppose," Harry had disappointment written all over his face. "Somehow I'd got the idea that it's a frozen specimen of the real thing."

"If frozen," Mrs. Ascroft remarked, "it would surely have thawed out by now?"

There was something so devastatingly logical about this observation that we all looked at each other. Yes, it would have thawed out by now—and if not then, the powerful, hot lights under which it now lay would surely finish the job.

"Might investigate further," Ascroft decided. "I'll test it for hardness, electronic content, and so forth."

So he began to enjoy himself with all kinds of complicated instruments. He was not what one would call a 'scientific dabbler,' by any means; rather, he had specialised knowledge on many subjects, which made him an invaluable expert when it came to the specimens of other worlds. But here, for once, Ascroft was plainly up against it.

"Its atomic weight is one-eight-four," he said presently, "which puts it in the same class as our element eighty-five, which is tungsten. Tungsten is one of our hardest substances, of course, and an excellent conductor of electrical current. But why a once-living creature should be made up of such weird and immensely strong substance has me baffled."

There was silence for a moment amongst us, then I said: "We might as well leave it for the experts to work out. Not that I mean that as a slight on you, Mr. Ascroft—but as far as we are concerned, we're just wasting time."

Ascroft nodded. "I quite agree. I'm sure you must have lots more to tell us about Mercury, Harry, so let's get back to the lounge. I'll just switch off these floods, then we...."

Ascroft stopped speaking. He had turned towards the bench as he spoke—where the specimen from Mercury now lay—and now the reason for his truncation of words was obvious.

The thing from Mercury had moved...very slightly!

I cannot say why the sight of that queer string of cotton reels suddenly twitching should fill me with momentary panic—but it did. Simultaneously, I felt Lucy's hand gripping my arm. Glancing at her, I saw her dark eyes fixed on the specimen with rigid intensity.

Ascroft frowned and held up a hand for us to make no move. His wife complacently watched, not in the least disturbed. Harry Dagenham took a step forward, and then checked himself. It was clear from his expression that he was utterly dumbfounded by the fact that the imagined dead object was undergoing resurrection.

"Better watch out," Ascroft murmured. "We haven't the least idea how this thing may react if it comes wholly to life—"

The words were hardly out of his mouth before the thing did come wholly to life. From mere twitchings, it changed to undulating movement—or, more exactly, it behaved just as though a thrill were passing through it. It—it vibrated. Yes, that's the word. Have you ever watched a harp wire gradually coming to a standstill after it has been sharply struck? Well, that is how this 'something' from Mercury appeared to us. And at the same time, a soft glow appeared to pervade it, after the fashion of a glowworm.

"If you switched off those floods we'd be able to see if it really is alight," Lucy pointed out.

Ascroft nodded and moved silently to the switch

panel, his eyes never leaving the specimen. This was where his training as an explorer of the unknown revealed itself again: he never turned his back on a potential or actual enemy.

Reaching the panel he put out his hand to the 'make-and-break,' and in that instant the most incredible thing happened. The specimen flashed into the air as though it were made of steel spring. In a movement so quick it was impossible to follow it as it darted for Ascroft's hand. Thank heaven he was watching the specimen all the time, for he had just time to snatch his hand away when the horror crashed into the switch panel. What was more, it went clean through it! The ebonite facing was as clean-drilled as though with a machine cutter, and beyond lay a black hole and tangle of wires. One of the flood lamps instantly died out, its wires severed, but the remaining one blazed on steadily.

"My God!" Ascroft whispered, and perspiration was standing out in gleaming drops on his forehead.

"In heaven's name, what is it?" came Lucy's voice, in a dreadful whisper. "Did—did you see the way it went through that board?"

"Where is it now?" Harry Dagenham demanded, striding forward. "We've got to find it and kill it!"

Reaching the switchboard he peered into the hole the specimen had made; then Ascroft whirled him back.

"What the devil are you trying to do, Harry? Commit suicide? Don't you realise that that thing is completely lethal?"

"Seems to be, yes, but— We can't leave it running

wild!"

"Best thing to do is get out of here quickly," Mrs. Ascroft said, turning towards the door.

The suggestion was more than reasonable—but it was not to be. Before Mrs. Ascroft actually reached the door a blurred haze of pearly light streaked from behind the damaged switchboard and landed on the floor close beside the door, sending us all stumbling backwards in alarm.

Then we dared to look, gripping one another meanwhile. In absorbed fascination we stared at this horror of the innermost world, this fantastic object which looked like cotton reels held together by wires—and now we saw differences. For one thing the eyes were open and blazed at us with the ferocious intensity of blood-red rubies. The awful mouth was also partly gaping and, as I had surmised earlier, it made two halves of the head. There did not seem to be any sign of teeth; nor were there any evidences of beating pulses. The whole thing was an enigma, possessed of incredible speed and, possibly, death-dealing qualities.

"How do we get out?" came Lucy's frantic whisper. "Can't we scare it off somehow?"

"The biggest problem is how it comes to be alive!" Harry Dagenham was standing with his fists clenched, his eyes fixed on the glowing length. "Any ideas, Mr. Ascroft?"

"Only thing I can think of is that it is a form of life which can remain in indefinite suspended animation. Perhaps, even, it actually thrives on the sunlit side of Mercury but goes into hibernation as soon as the planet's slow rotation moves it into the night hemisphere. There the space-frost laid it out, and there it remained—before you happened to find it, Harry. Now it has revived!"

"I can see that, sir, but why such a long delay? It has been in the specimen box for quite a time, and the temperature more or less normal—"

"Wait!" Ascroft exclaimed. "I have it. Until it was subjected to all those vibrations and electrical radiations nothing happened; then after that, it began to recover. It wasn't warmth which brought it back to life: it was electrical energy."

"You mean the horror feeds on electricity?" Lucy gasped.

"Looks like it," I told her. "It's not so fantastic as it sounds, either. Any form of life connected with Mercury must of necessity be highly electrical in nature, because the whole of Mercury is soaked in solar radiations."

"That's right," Harry confirmed.

Silence dropped on us again. We were at an impasse. That red-eyed horror barred the way to the door, and we were scared to make a move in case it flew at us. Finally it was the forthright Harry.

"Be damned to this! What kind of weaklings are we to be dictated to by an infernal length of cotton reels? I'm going to have a smack at it, sir!"

"Doing what?" Ascroft's voice was curt with anxiety.

For answer Harry turned slowly, keeping his eyes

on the object, and felt around on the shelf above the bench nearby until he had contacted the heavy bottle containing sulphuric acid. Lifting it down he weighed it in his hand—then with a sudden quick swing he flung the entire bottle and contents straight at the thing beside the door.

It was astounding how fast that thing could travel. One moment it was there; the next it had vanished. Even a mouse would have seemed to dawdle beside this greased lightning Certainly it was missing when the acid fumed and smoked from the shattered bottle. All of them stumbled away from the acrid fumes and the bubbling corrosive on the floor,

"Blast!" Harry muttered direfully, glaring around him. "Where did it go?"

"Never mind that!" Lucy panted. "The door's clear, so let's be going—"

Mrs. Ascroft was there before her, quickly grasping the handle. She had only just done so when a living bolt exploded straight across the laboratory from a far corner. It hit Mrs. Ascroft in the back and in one second of time went clean through her! I never saw anything so horrifying or so fantastic. The poor woman just did not stand a chance. She stood for a second, a burned hole gaping in her dress at the back; then without uttering a sound she collapsed limply amidst the streams of acid and broken glass lying on the floor.

By this time the horror from Mercury had vanished again, but since the door was in one piece it was assumed that it—the thing from Mercury—was still in the laboratory somewhere. At the moment we had almost forgotten about it. Our whole attention was upon the stricken Mrs. Ascroft.

Somehow we managed to drag her from the midst of the glass and acid and laid her dead form on the bench, Ascroft himself elbowing precious instruments out of the way to make room for her. For several seconds he stood looking at the frozen expression of terror on his wife's dead face, then he swung round, his jaw taut.

"Try and get out if you can," he ordered. "I'm going to deal with this devilish thing myself! Either it will die or I shall! I'm going to—"

"No you're not, sir," Harry snapped, clenching his big fists. "Anyway, I'm staying with you to help. I'm responsible for the specimen, anyhow. The rest of you had better go."

"The 'rest of us' merely comprises Lucy and myself," I said quietly. "You don't suppose I'm going to run out, do you? But you'd better go, Lucy—"

"And stay out there alone not knowing—?" Her dark eyes fixed on me in horror. "No, I couldn't do it, Duncan! I couldn't!"

"There are servants in the house, Lucy; you won't be alone."

I compressed my lips and held her tightly against me. "All right, if that's the way you want it. But it could—and probably will—mean death for the lot of us before we're finished. You realise that?"

"I'm stopping!" Lucy declared stubbornly—and that was that.

With a great effort Ascroft forced himself to be calm. How he did it I don't know, for the grief and horror that must have been trying to overwhelm him would have flattened most men.

"That thing," he said, "is basically *energy*! I'm pretty well sure of it now. Nothing else could move so fast, or so completely through solids—and through flesh and blood." He gave a brief glance towards his dead wife. "You said a while ago, Duncan, that any form of life connected with Mercury must of necessity be electrical. You're right—but energy is the correct term. That snakelike horror is nothing more or less than pure energy, a form of life that we had never encountered before. Where we breathe in air and exhale carbon dioxide, this fantastic object absorbs electricity and gives forth energy, or something like it. It's a product of solar energy, diabolical beyond imagining, and possessing a certain low form of intelligence.... I have the feeling it won't go very far from here, because it can feed on the many electrical currents connected with this laboratory—"

"How right you are!" Harry Dagenham whispered. "Come and take a look at this!"

Whilst Ascroft had been speaking I had noticed Harry had crossed over to the hole in the switchboard. Now he was peering through it, attentively watching something within. Cautiously we moved to his side. We had by now become so fascinated by the thing from Mercury that it outweighed our horror of Mrs. Ascroft's death.

Then, abruptly, we all beheld the Mercutian horror. Its vice-like mouth was snipped onto the main power cable at the back of the switchboard and judging from the rippling vibrations passing through its body it was feeding steadily on the current.

"It's damnable!" Harry whispered. "Whoever saw a form of life like that!"

"Cut off the current!" Lucy urged. "Without nourishment it'll die—or should."

Ascroft hesitated, then shook his head. "Not just yet. That thing seems to instinctively know when the current is going to be switched off, which is probably why it flew at me when I reached to that make-and-break contact for the floods. Also, when my wife reached to the doorknob, there she was close to the light switch as well. This thing must again have assumed that power was going to be cut out— But enough of this! We've got to kill it somehow. Let's think now. What can we use...?"

"There's mercury fulminate on the shelf there," Harry said. "Give it to me and I'll soon—"

"And blow us to Hades as well?" Ascroft shook his head. "No, that won't do. We've got to think of something else!"

But what? This was what set us looking at each other, with an occasional covert glance towards Mrs. Ascroft. Ascroft himself, apparently still in control of his emotions, was lost in thought, then he glanced towards the doorway.

"If somehow I could get out of here—or rather if all

of us could get out of here—we could cut off the electricity at the mains. It might starve the thing."

"I doubt it," Harry Dagenham said, with a grim glance. "If it fails to find enough sustenance in here, it will start looking elsewhere. Only logical, isn't it? That means it'll bore through the wall and escape either into the house or the open,"

"If into the open we at least would be safe," Lucy pointed out.

"Yes, but...." Harry scowled worriedly. "We just can't let a thing like that loose on the unprepared community! It'd wreak murder everywhere it went."

I had not been taking much notice of the conversation for the simple reason that I was trying to think of a way out of our predicament, and it seemed to me that I *had* thought of something. Water! Or moisture of some kind! If the thing was basically electrical, then would not water blow it up, or short-circuit it, or something? Immediately the idea dawned on me I passed it on to the still hesitating Ascroft.

"Could be," he admitted, his eyes brightening. "No harm in trying. Keep a watch on that damned thing, if you can, whilst I get across to the sink."

He moved silently, reached the sink without mishap and proceeded to fill a small enamel jug with water. The rest of us divided our attention between him and the horror from Mercury, still feasting on the electric current.

"Here we go!" Ascroft muttered, his face taut, and after taking careful aim he flung the jug's contents through the hole in the switch-panel. At the same moment Lucy and Harry Dagenham threw themselves backwards, but I could not resist remaining to see what happened.

Nothing did—or at least nothing spectacular. Have you ever seen how water flashes into globules and explodes on a red-hot plate? Such was the effect here. Either the Mercutian 'snake' was extremely hot, or else the energy it emitted amounted to the same thing; but certainly moisture had no chance to seize upon it. Amidst a faint vapour of dispersing steam the object went on feasting undisturbed.

"This," Ascroft said, white-faced with harassment, "demands a plan of campaign, and we're fighting a ruthless, implacable enemy which can move with the speed of lightning. It's agreed we've got to get out of here by that door?"

Harry and I nodded, but not Lucy. Instead she glanced at the main window through which the night sky was visible

"Why not try it?" she suggested. "There's no light-switch or power contact near the window, so maybe we'd get away with it."

"I'll make the first move," Harry Dagenham decided, but before he did so, he searched around until he found a cast iron spanner nearly three feet long. Normally it was used for turning off the laboratory's water stop-tap, but it made an excellent weapon just the same.

"How's it doing?" Harry asked, glancing towards the switch-panel—and Lucy tiptoed to have a look.

"Still feasting."

Harry nodded briefly and vaulted up onto the bench, quickly unfastening the window. Then from behind that switchboard there came a sudden violent convulsion of movement. Petrified, we all stared as that glowing length of 'cotton reels' vomited through the hole in the panel and flashed across the laboratory to where Harry was standing on the bench. Not for an instant did he lose his head. He ducked, superbly timing it so that the horror flew over his head with a couple of inches clearance. It struck the wall violently and left a zigzagged scorch mark, then, fast as light itself, it zipped around and came back.

Up went Harry's spanner and, again calculating it perfectly he slammed the spanner down with all the power of his muscles. Snake and spanner collided at the same instant and across Harry's face there flashed a numbed look of intolerable pain. As though he himself had been hit, he came tumbling from the bench and landed flat on his face on the laboratory floor.

As for the spanner, it broke in two! Yes, broke in two. Things happened so fast it was hard to follow them, but I did notice that as the spanner landed dead centre upon the Mercutian horror's back there was a bright flash and the horror darted clear, leaving a bisected spanner to clang down onto the bench. Apparently, though, the thing had been somewhat hurt, for it was flying around in blind darts and lunges, colliding with the walls and sending cascades of sparks flashing from metallic instruments.... Then, gradually, it became quiescent again in a far corner, its baleful ruby eyes fixed upon us.

"That thing is either inconceivably hard, or else it emits a shell of energy which is disintegrative to anything touching it."

Ascroft made this observation after a moment or two; then he, Lucy and I began to back warily to where Harry was lying on the floor. It only took us a moment or two to discover that he was not dead—just knocked out with some kind of shock.

"Probably the thing's electricity travelled up his arm," Lucy suggested, and Ascroft and I merely nodded, not knowing whether she was anywhere near right or not.

As a matter of fact she was—or so Harry said as he gradually came round.

"Kick like a mule." he muttered, massaging his shoulder. "Like hitting a bar of iron with a stick. Nearly split my palm.... On top of that there was an electric jolt which blacked me out for a moment...." His eyes wandered towards the 'thing' still in the corner. "I'll get the damned thing yet," he breathed. "Sort of duty, really. I brought it here and I'll dispose of it."

"You hope." Lucy remarked uneasily; then she glanced up at the unlatched window. "Doesn't seem as though we're going to get out that way.... Wonder how it knew what we were going to do?"

"Because it is intelligent and able to reason things out," Ascroft answered. "I'm arriving at a pretty surprising conclusion concerning this string of electrified bobbins. I think it is not so much a specimen of Mercutian reptile life as a genuine Mercutian. In other words, as much a thinking, reasoning inhabitant of Mercury as we are of Earth. Life on Mercury, forever drenched in solar tides and energies, *could* be like that, you know."

"I suppose...it could." Harry sounded as though the words were being dragged out of him. He was standing up now, supporting his big, muscular body against the bench whilst he fully recovered.

"If it is a form of intelligent life, why does it have to be so ferocious?" Lucy questioned. "One would think that, having the power of reason—as it certainly has—it would be willing to try and communicate with us."

"One can still have reasoning power and yet be savage," Harry pointed out. "Look at some of the uncivilised tribes of our own world. They're brutal, murdering sadists—yet they have the gift of reason, same as any human beings. This may be something similar."

"Reverse the positions," Ascroft murmured. "If a savage of Earth were trapped on another world by beings of superior intelligence, what would he do? Use every physical power to destroy them. This creature, or thing, or whatever it is, may be trying to do the same to us."

"If it can reason," Lucy said deliberately, "it must know that if we escape it will be left to itself, so why does it try and stop us getting out? We thought earlier it mistook our effort at opening the laboratory door as an attempt to cut off the power. This time it could not have thought that, because the window's miles away from a power switch."

"It's just plain, blind ferocious!" Harry snapped. "It's a killer—and nothing else. If we don't destroy it, it will destroy us, and that's the top and bottom of the issue!"

Again the silence dropped, faced as we were with this impossible situation. Finally, it was Harry who again started speaking.

"If we could somehow manoeuvre it into the vice there, do you think it would destroy the vice, or could it be crushed?"

"From the way it behaves, I'd say it would destroy the vice," Ascroft replied. "In any case, Harry, that's a mad idea. We'll never tempt it to destruction: it's too wary for that."

"Why do you always have to think of destroying things?" Lucy demanded, surprisingly. "Ever think what a bit of reasoning might do? It may understand mathematics, if not language. I assume mathematics must be the same no matter what part of the universe in which they're applied."

"Reciting the multiplication table to this brute isn't going to help a bit," I said gruffly. "Our best move, whilst it's stuck in the corner there, is to make a dash for the door—and I mean *now*!"

I did not waste any time, either. The very second I finished speaking I flung myself across the laboratory, grabbed the door handle, and twisted it. Instantly that hurtling horror dived for me, but I had time to see it coming. I ducked, and the infernal thing went straight through the door itself and into the passageway beyond.

"Shut the door!" Ascroft yelled. "We'll go out through the window!"

He darted for the bench and I made to slam the door—but at that same instant the Mercutian snake shot back again, making a second hole in the door. Obviously it was aiming straight for Ascroft, and there was just plain nothing that Lucy, Harry, or myself could do about it.

Appalled, we watched. Standing up on the bench as he was, straddling his dead wife, in fact, Ascroft was the perfect target. The flying bolt of energy struck him— And that was that. I jerked my head away, grabbed blindly at Lucy, and together we lurched out into the passage. Harry came after us, slamming the laboratory door. We stood breathing hard, fearful, expecting every moment that the thing would come flying at us through the damaged door.

When it did not, we began to get something of a grip on ourselves again. We gave each other quick glances in the light being dimly reflected from the hall.

"Do we go back and see what happened to Ascroft?" I asked, but Harry shook his big head.

"Not damned likely! We know exactly what would happen to him—same as to his wife. No flesh and blood can stand up against a thing like that. For God's sake, let's get into the lounge. We all need a drink."

Once we landed in the lounge, Harry fixed us up with bracers. We drank them down, felt better, then looked at one another. By this time it was close on 11:15, and the summer night had completely shut down.

"We'd better warn the servants," I said abruptly. "No telling when that thing may break loose into the house itself."

"And I'll cut off the mains," Harry decided; but before he had reached the lounge door, Lucy called him.

"Just a minute, Harry! If you cut off the power, that thing is liable to start wandering around looking for more juice from somewhere. Better not do that—"

Lucy stopped with a little gasp. The reason was obvious—for the lights had suddenly extinguished themselves. It seemed to me that I had heard a remote bang—probably the main fuse blown.

"That damned thing must have chewed through the power wire in the laboratory," Harry said quickly, returning to us in the gloom.

Before I could answer him, there came a tap on the lounge door and Jackson, the Ascroft's manservant, appeared. In one hand he was carrying a lighted candle.

"Begging your pardon...." He paused, obviously at a loss. He had been intending to address Ascroft, no doubt, and instead beheld our three grim and probably frightened faces.

"I know, the fuses have gone." I said, speaking for all of us. "Matter of fact, Jackson, there's trouble in the laboratory. Take my advice and leave the house at once, along with the rest of the domestics."

"But, sir, I couldn't possibly do that without Mr.

Ascroft's express instructions—"

"Mr. Ascroft will never give any more instructions!" Lucy burst out desperately. "He's dead! Killed! And so is Mrs. Ascroft! There's something horrible loose in the laboratory!"

Jackson was plainly shocked, but he was not shaken. Unlike us, he had not yet seen the horror from Mercury so he could manage to keep his nerve.

"That being the case, sir," he said finally, peering at me, "what do I do? Phone the police?"

"No." I shook my head. "They couldn't do anything. You have the best advice I can give you, Jackson—Get out as fast as you can."

Jackson hesitated, then: "With all due respect, sir, I cannot see that the emergency is so great, otherwise you, Miss Clinton, and Mr. Dagenham would surely have gone yourselves by now? I feel it incumbent on me to discover what has happened to the master and mistress."

"Don't be a damned fool!" Harry yelled at him, as he turned towards the door. "Once you're in that laboratory, you're finished—and ourselves too, probably."

"I'm sorry, sir, but I still consider it my duty to examine the position more closely."

With that he turned away and left us in the dark. There was the sound of Harry's hard breathing.

"What the devil does he think we are? A bunch of criminals who've killed Mr. and Mrs. Ascroft for some obscure reason?"

"He's simply being loyal to them," Lucy sighed.

"Can't blame him for that."

"We can't go on like this," Harry said presently. "Just waiting for something to happen. Either we kill that blasted thing, or else get hold of somebody who can."

"Neither police nor fire brigade can help us here—" I started to say; then I was interrupted by a sudden splintering of glass.

We looked about us in the darkness. The sound had come from outside somewhere.

"Only glass there is out there belongs to the garage windows," Harry said abruptly. "Better take a look—"

He led the way to the French windows and yanked back the curtains. Pale starlight showed where the windows stood, and beyond them was the expanse of grounds, which entirely encircled the residence. A little to the right lay the stables, now converted into a big private garage, but if there was anything wrong there we were too far away to observe it.

"Begging your pardon, sir—" Flickering yellow came into the gloom and we twirled around to behold Jackson. He looked ghastly in the uncertain light. but as far as we could tell was unharmed.

"Well?" Harry asked harshly. "Did you see the lab?"

"Yes, sir. I—er—am not quite sure *what* I saw. Something luminous smashed against the window and escaped outside. I stayed long enough to look at the master and mistress.... I mean the *late* master and mistress and...."

"So it escaped outside, did it?" Harry's eyes were

bright in the candlelight. "That must have been the glass we heard."

"No! I'm sure it wasn't." Lucy shook her head emphatically. "The sound we heard came from directly over there!" She indicated the garage. "The laboratory window is behind us from here: we'd never hear it break. That thing is in the garage. I'm sure of it."

"Might I ask, sir, what it is?" Jackson enquired, and I told him briefly.

"Which makes it necessary for you and the servants to get away from here," I insisted. "We—that is Mr. Dagenham and I will do what we can to kill that brute, but if we fail, we'll have to run for it too and advise the police that it's running wild."

"And what do I do?" Lucy demanded.

"Go with Jackson and the others. You'll be safer. This is no job for a girl to be mixed up in!"

"I'm staying!" Lucy said flatly. "I told you that earlier, and it still goes. As I said, I couldn't stand the suspense of not knowing what was happening to you."

"I, too, sir, shall stay," Jackson decided, becoming his normal immovable self. "I shall not inform the rest of the servants, since the danger has now receded from the house itself. In any case, most of them have retired by now. It appears that our quarry is in the garage, and it is to there that we must carry the attack!"

Harry laughed shortly. "Using what weapons? Water doesn't affect it—and as for trying to deal it a blow, it's impossible. I don't think bullets would make any difference either. It is a form of living energy and therefore, far as we know, quite beyond normal means of extinction."

"Of that, sir, I am none too sure. I noticed, in the brief glimpse I had of that object in the laboratory that it emits something resembling lightning from head and tail—which bears out your theory of it being electrical. Therefore, the obvious way to destroy it is to short-circuit it."

"Just like that!" I remarked dryly.

"I feel, sir, that the notion is based on logic." Jackson put the candlestick down on the table and surveyed us in sanctimonious calm. "What has really brought the idea to my mind is the fact that the fuses have blown in the meter."

"I don't see the connection," Harry grunted.

"It is this, sir. The fuses have blown because the current has short-circuited."

"Through that thing eating through the laboratory power wire," I confirmed. "Right—we're with you so far."

"If no fuses had been placed there, the wires would have burned themselves out. Correct?"

"What has this to do with the Mercutian thing?" I demanded.

"Simply this sir. That creature is evidently a sort of living power wire, generating its own energy. That energy escapes from its head and tail, which is probably the equivalent of our method of breathing."

"Could be," Harry agreed, plainly surprised. "You talk more like a scientist than a manservant, Jackson."

"My father was a scientist, sir, and I have a natural inkling. I also feel that I am in the position of being the looker-on who sees most of the fight. You have tried water and physical violence without success. In the former case, the heat of the object probably explains why the water had no effect: it is blasted into steam before it can do its work. In the case of normal electricity, there is no heat as such: here we have the immense heat begotten of the generation of energy. Physical blows fail because the energy is equivalent to an iron-hard shell. Hence the need of a short-circuit."

"But how?" Harry was nearly dancing with impatience. "*How*, man?"

"By placing head to tail, sir, and seeing it stays there even if only for a second or two."

"What!" I exclaimed blankly, for at first sound it seemed like the suggestion of a lunatic.

"Imagine the Mercutian thing to be a power wire, filled with electrical energy generated by some mysterious process within itself. If you bent that wire and allowed both ends to touch, the whole wire would melt and be destroyed—the old short-circuit principle. So it should be here, I imagine. It is like suffocating an atmosphere breather by imprisoning it in its own carbon-dioxide exhalation."

"In other words," Lucy said, her simplicity leading her straight to the point, "you mean *fuse* it?"

"Exactly, madam. If the outflow of energy has nowhere to go and is automatically turned back on itself, it can only destroy the 'carrier' of the energy, which in this case is the object itself. If it were just a wire, a fuse would blow instead."

"I think," Harry said, pondering, "that you've really got something there, Jackson."

"Thank you, sir. That being so, I see nothing to be gained by delaying any further. It would appear that our quarry is in the garage over there."

So the four of us went silently across the space to the main garage doors and stood looking at them. Now we were close up, we could see that one of the frosted windows had been smashed in pieces. Very cautiously I peered through the empty framework, but all appeared to be dark beyond.

"No signs," I murmured. "And anyway I can't see what the 'thing' would want in here, anyhow!"

"There are three cars garaged in here, sir," Jackson pointed out. "Every one of them in good running order—which also means that their batteries must be well up. My guess is that the 'thing,' failing to secure nourishment after the power failure, instinctively sensed the batteries and settled on those."

"Nauseating thought," Harry muttered, "but probably right all the same."

"Look," Lucy said urgently. "We just can't walk in here and hope for the best. We've got to have some kind of plan to deal with the thing. If we don't, it'll probably kill us before we even know what's happened!"

We were silent for a moment, assessing the situation. From within the garage there came no sounds. Then Harry abruptly snapped his fingers.

"A little while ago I got the idea that if we could get the thing in a vice and crush the life out of it we might win—but Mr. Ascroft seemed to think the vice itself would be destroyed."

"I think, sir," Jackson said, after a moment, "that your idea should be wedded to mine. There is a vice of the large variety in the garage there: that much I know. Now, if we could trap the 'thing' in it, it could be held steady whilst its nose and tail were forced to touch each other!"

"Very nice theory but hopeless in practice," I pointed out. "For one thing, it's quite impossible to get hold of that thing without receiving a fatal electric shock—and anyway, it moves so fast that it's impossible to get hold of it; and for another, we can't get it anywhere near the vice unless we do get hold of it. The thing's a vicious circle."

Jackson was not unduly disturbed. "Handling things electrical merely requires sufficient insulation, Mr. Dagenham. In the late master's laboratory there are various pairs of gloves, which he used for his experiments with the lesser cyclotron. They might be proof enough when handling the 'thing'."

"It's lunacy!" I declared flatly.

"Possibly so, sir," Jackson admitted, "but there's no other way. I'll go along to the laboratory and see what I can find."

When Jackson came into view again, he had not only got several pairs of enormous insulated gloves but also four protective suits, evidently used for work in radioactivity. He had dumped the whole lot in a rubber-wheeled barrow, which he now set down on its shafts outside the garage doors.

"At least I think we can have adequate protection from the 'thing's' energy with what we have here," he announced. "I do not anticipate, though, that it will enable us to withstand its deadly lunges. We shall have to hope for the best."

It seemed to me, as I struggled into one of the suits, that Jackson was either a very brave man, or else he just seemed that way because he had had no practical demonstration yet of the Mercutian creature's fury. Whichever was the answer, he had become the leader of our little quartet, and it was he who finally led the way by reaching inside the broken garage window and unfastening the door catch from the inside. Then, one by one—Lucy coming in last—we crept into the darkness and Jackson closed the doors behind us.

"The closed doors might act as a deterrent to the creature escaping," came his muffled voice from within the hood.

"Whereabouts is the vice?" I asked him quickly, and he nodded in its direction. I could only see his movement very dimly by the star shine through the skylight, but in a second or two I managed to discern where the bench, and presumably the vice, lay.

Then we began a wary advance. Since there were three cars, it meant that there were two side 'aisles' and two centre ones—one for each of us. So presently we met again beside the gleaming radiator of the centremost car—and at the same time we saw 'it'. It was in the engine of the car nearest the wall. A gaping hole had been smashed through the bonnet, and through the gap we could discern that soft, elusive glow that betrayed the 'thing's' presence.

"To get it to the bench and the vice without exposing ourselves to danger, we need a counter-attraction," came Jackson's murmuring voice. "Something electrical."

"Another battery," Harry responded. "Nothing else will do it. When it's sucked all the juice out of that one it'll look for some more. Take a long time maybe, but it's worth trying."

"Take it from this nearer car here," I suggested—and immediately we went to work as silently as possible.

Apparently, though, the creature was not particularly concerned whether we were present or not—and it must certainly have known that we were there, because to move the battery from a car in absolute silence just is not possible. With four of us at work, we made comparative simplicity of the job, and presently heaved the battery up between us and put it on the bench, jammed up closely beside the vice.

"Get it this far and we may manage to manhandle it the rest." Harry's muffled voice only just reached the rest of us. "And one other preparation, too...."

With his heavily gloved hand he unscrewed the vice's jaws about three inches and there for the moment we left things. According to our reckoning there must come a time when the 'thing' would come this way, seize on the battery, and then—

"Would it do any good," Lucy asked, "to switch on the engine of the car where the thing is now? It would start the dynamo and charge the battery. Wouldn't the sudden shock either kill or paralyze the beastly thing, leeched onto the battery as it is?"

"If it did anything at all, it would probably stimulate it," I answered. "Once the dynamo got going, the battery would start to charge and give our nasty little friend an 'extra helping' of nourishment. No, nothing we can do but wait."

And this we did, in a far corner of the garage. What time it was, we none of us knew, because it was impossible to get at our watches. It was probably around midnight when we began the vigil, and it seemed as though hours passed before the 'thing' at last made a move.

As usual, it did it with lightning velocity, suddenly shooting through the hole in the car bonnet and then commencing a flashing, darting investigation against walls and roofs. We crouched and waited silently—and abruptly it seemed to become aware of us. Straight as an arrow it came hurtling towards us— We surged, shifted, and broke apart.

Jackson got the worst of it. The damnable thing went through his suit, and through him, like a white-hot needle. In a matter of seconds Jackson was sprawling on the concrete floor, obviously finished. Meantime, the 'thing' appeared to be flying around and gathering velocity to attack the rest of us.

"Quick—into this car!" Lucy's voice gasped. "It might save us!"

She staggered forward, dragged open the rear door, and tumbled into the upholstery beyond. Harry Dagenham followed her and I came last. I was only just in time too. The hurtling bolt of living energy struck the glass top of the door as I closed it. Splintering powder marks spread over it, but it did not break.

Unsatisfied, the Mercutian horror plunged again. The impact it made against the car roof sounded as though a small bomb had hit us—but fortunately the all-steel chassis prevented the 'thing' from smashing its way through. It tried again, but not in the same place, and still the roof held.

"If it *does* get through, and in this confined space, it's the finish," Lucy panted. "Maybe it wasn't so smart to come in here after all."

"So help me, I'm not standing for this any longer," Harry Dagenham muttered, clenching his huge gloved fists. "We're just running away from the damned thing, hiding in terror before it! Okay for you two, because you're not responsible for this fiendish thing being turned loose—but *I* am, and I'm going to do something about it."

Before we could stop him, he had pushed the rear door open and clambered out again into the garage. Lucy and I made no effort to follow him: we just hadn't the courage. But Harry—well, he stood there, dimly visible in the star shine through the skylight, the cowl-like helmet of his suit turning as he looked about him.

Then, with a screaming flash the Mercutian dived for him from nowhere. He ducked, getting accustomed to it by this time, and then stumbled to the bench. Tensely, Lucy and I watched his dim figure—and time and again he dodged out of the direct line of impact as the Mercutian power-dived upon him. Suddenly Lucy and I had to jerk our eyes away as intense blue white flame gushed into being, filling the garage with the livid, pitiless glare of burning magnesium powder. In a second or two we grasped the situation. Harry was beside the bench with a small-type oxy-acetylene welder in his hand. We couldn't look at him because of the glare, but we could hear his enraged voice.

"Come on, damn you! Tackle this if you dare! It'll go through you quicker than you can go through it!"

"This is too much for me," I said abruptly, gripping Lucy's gloved hand. "I'm going to open this door and we can watch round the edge of it: that way the car will hide the glare of his welder."

My guess was right, and from there on Lucy and I peered down the narrow 'aisle' towards the bench, only closing our eyes as the welder's blinding glare swam occasionally into our vision. For the rest of the time Harry stood there, looking gigantic in his protective suiting, swinging the white-hot core of flame towards the 'thing' every time it darted towards him. And, gradually, we could see that Harry was using a certain strategy.

It was plain that the Mercutian horror was afraid of the flame, probably realizing that here was something hotter than anything it could itself generate. And, by degrees, secure in having found a weapon at last, Harry contrived to force the darting, and even bewildered 'snake' into the angle between the two walls. In this area there also lay the bench end where stood the vice.

Then, just at the vital moment, when it seemed Harry had the thing pinpointed so he could turn the full blaze of the welder upon it, the oxy-acetylene gas tank emptied itself. The blinding glare died to the yellow of an ordinary gas burner and Harry gave a yelp of fury.

The 'thing' twisted and writhed violently in the corner into which heat, flame, and fear had driven it. Harry dropped the jet of yellow flame to the bench and then lunged forward.

His next act made Lucy and I stare in petrified horror.

He closed his great, gloved hands above the deadly creature and wrestled relentlessly with it as it fought and squirmed to break free. In the sombre yellow of the dying gas flame Harry looked like a futuristic fisherman holding onto an electric eel—but it was an undoubted fact that his immense strength and the insulation of his suit and gloves—combined with the Mercutian 'thing's' weakness through terror—was giving him the mastery.

Fighting, gasping, swearing, he forced the squirming horror to the vice and there held it by main strength.

"Some help quick!" he yelled. "Tighten the vice!"

I tumbled out of the car and blundered to his aid.

With fumbling fingers I tightened up the vice—tighter and tighter yet until at last the writhing, glowing monstrosity was held immovably, electrical energy flashing from his lashing tail and darting head.

"Got it!" Harry whispered. "Now it's my turn—!"

He hunched forward, gripped head and tail in either hand, then with his muscles taut forced the two extremities gradually towards each other. His iron strength won, and at last the two ends touched. There was a blinding flash, a cloud of smoke, and darkness. Then Lucy came stealing out of the gloom and gripped my arm.

"Good for Jackson," Harry said at last, dragging off his helmet. "His theory was right! And if that was the kind of life Mercury breeds, it's a planet best left well alone!"

# THE WORLD THAT DISSOLVED

## Chapter 1: Observatory Ten

Curt Vernol slowly cut off the power of his flyer's rear jets, gave a burst of recoil to the forward rockets, which immediately slowed down the little spaceship's tremendous headlong rush through infinity, a rush it had pretty well maintained ever since leaving Earth. Now it was in the remote regions far beyond Pluto.

Somewhat moodily, Curt gazed, through the forward port. To the left hung little Pluto. Dead ahead, still some 300,000 miles distant, loomed a lone planetoid—actually the outermost body on which mankind had so far set foot. A lonely little world, only a third the size of Earth.

A world utterly deserted save for one massive completely airtight observatory, better known as Observatory Ten, furthest flung observation post of all the system.

Curt's eyes became faintly disgusted as he studied the tiny world.

"So that's where I've got to spend twelve months!"

he growled. "Twelve months on a spatial desert island, keeping a watch on the cosmos for the long distance ships, guiding their courses.... A veritable celestial lighthouse! Charming!"

Inwardly cursing the day he had joined the Space Observers and thereby left himself open for lonely jobs of this sort, he gave a final burst to the rockets and swept downward at terrific speed toward the distant planetoid. He hung tight in his seat, eating up the dozens of miles.... In two hours the lonely world was below him, jagged and scarred.

He flattened the ship out, made a perfect landing on the flat plain within a mile of the massive, towering Observatory.

In a moment he had scrambled into his spacesuit, and opened the airlock. Carefully he trod onto the jagged rock of the palely lit world, waiting with infinite caution to avoid the slightest chance of tearing his suit. The light of the ridiculous sun, shedding the equivalent of full moonlight on Earth, enabled him to see pretty clearly where he was going.

All around him crouched massive, rugged rocks, glinting faintly in the dim light. Overhead, the vast vault of the universe was dusted with multimillions of stars.... Curt felt a trifle depressed, realized he would need all his willpower to defeat the loneliness begotten of constant association with cosmic fastness....

At last he arrived at the monstrous airlock of the Observatory, paused for a moment to survey the rearing walls of glazite, an isotopic metal of beryllium basis.

Far atop the building loomed the solitary unbreakable glass dome through which the observations were made.

He smiled rather grimly to himself, then reached out with his heated glove and pressed the lock's external button. He waited as the outermost lock began to move sideways, then he stepped inside. Three locks in all, the centremost one a 'levelling off' room wherein he removed his spacesuit and accustomed himself to normal air pressure and a 70° Fahrenheit temperature....

As the last lock opened, he stepped into the huge major room of the observatory and silently faced the man he had come to relieve.

Curt had never particularly liked Fletcher Gaunt at any time, and so far as he could see the twelve-month interval had not improved the man in the least. He was still coldly supercilious, bitter-eyed, with a permanently harsh tautness about his thin-lipped mouth. Certainly he looked in good health. His lean cheeks were tinged with colour, his black hair stood up vitally....

For several seconds he stood regarding Curt steadily, then he snapped out uncivilly.

"And what the hell do you want?"

Curt stared at him in surprise. "What do I want? Your time's up, that's all: I'm here to relieve you. I thought you'd be glad to see me."

"I'm not glad to see you, and my time isn't up for another week," Gaunt retorted acidly. "I don't like people here before time, it disarranges my work. You've got to work to schedule here, stuck away in this blasted hole—and I don't like it being interrupted! See?"

Curt remained silent, his lips compressed. Gaunt waved his arm vaguely.

"I saw your ship land," he growled. "I thought you were a lone traveller in need of help. That's why I let the locks open."

"I travelled rather faster than I intended. That new Myers rocket fuel enabled me to knock a week off schedule...." Curt thrust his hands in his pockets, glanced around him. "I don't see what you're so concerned about, Gaunt. Why don't you get moving and hand things over to me? If I'm early, that's to your advantage."

"Yeah?" Gaunt eyed him darkly. "I'll go when I'm good and ready, not before. Nice damn thing when a guy can't finish his shift in peace! In another week I'll be glad to go, and not until then. In the meantime, it's against the Company's rules to have two men on one station, so you'd better be on your way."

Curt swung around, his brows down over his grey eyes.

"On my way! What the hell are you talking about?"

"Clear enough, isn't it? Besides, seven days' extra food will put you in the queer at the end of your shift here. My time isn't up yet, so cruise around until it is. That's all!"

Gaunt turned aside, only to swing back as Curt gripped his arm fiercely. Their eyes met.

"What's the big idea, Gaunt?" Curt asked in a low voice. "What are you afraid of? You don't think I'm mug enough to believe you're stopping here for love of duty, do you?"

"If you've any brains, that's just what you will believe!"

"Yeah? And suppose I just stick around to worry you?"

"In that case...." Gaunt shrugged—then, with a sudden lightning movement he snatched his flame pistol from its holster and levelled it steadily. "In that case," he resumed softly, "you'll meet up with the business end of this! Understand?"

Curt slowly raised his arms, eyes narrowed and jaw set. Gaunt came forward slowly, smiling cynically.

"I don't like little boys around before time, see? Either you take off into space again, or—"

He broke off suddenly as Curt abruptly lowered his right arm and slammed out his fist with terrific force. It struck Gaunt clean in the face, sent him reeling backwards with blood trickling from a split lip. Taken utterly by surprise, he went reeling backward, brought up hard against the control board of the monstrous telescopic reflector. His gun clattered out of his hand.

Instantly, Curt dived for it—but he wasn't quick enough. By the time he had slithered to it, Gaunt had recovered himself, snatched it up from the floor from under Curt's very hand. Ruthlessly he swung it upward and depressed the button....

Curt dropped with a crash to the floor, the upper part of his head entirely seared away. He dropped face up, still with an expression of amazed horror on his features.

For several seconds Gaunt stood staring, mechanically wiping his bleeding lip with the back of his hand. The gun fumes curled acridly round his nostrils.... Then very gradually he mastered himself, pushed the gun back in its holster.

"Damn!" he breathed, and scowled. "This may prove difficult unless I—"

He stood thinking for a while, then slowly nodded to himself. In a moment or two he had drawn a spacesuit onto the corpse, pulled on his own suit, then lifted the body in his arms. Opening the triple locks, he finally gained Curt's small space flyer and dropped the body inside it. He removed the spacesuit again, then taking Curt's own flame gun from his belt he fired a charge harmlessly into the air, put the weapon back in Curt's stiffening hand.

The rest was simple. He set the space machine's controls to a straight path and slipped the automatic delayed-action pilot in commission. By the time he had left the ship and closed the airlock with the external counter switches, the controls were ready to function.

Smiling grimly behind his glass helmet, Gaunt watched the little flyer hurtle upward, vanishing almost immediately against the star-scattered expanse of void.

"Easy," he murmured. "Suicide in the void. Common enough when loneliness gets a pilot, especially a new guy like Vernol.... Possibly he'll never be found. Even if he is, I'm in the clear."

Chuckling at his own ingenuity, he returned to the

observatory. Hardly had he removed his spacesuit before the long-distance space radio whistled stridently for attention. Immediately he settled before the banked apparatus, tuned in to the special wavelength, which was the secret of himself and few associates. As he had expected, the coldly-clipped voice of Ranvil Gates came into the loudspeaker.

"Gaunt? We're two million miles away from you. All set for a landing when we arrive?"

"I am—now," Gaunt assented.

"Meaning what?"

Briefly Gaunt related the details of his adventure with Curt Vernol. Ranvil Gates gave a whistle.

"Say, that was a darned good idea of yours. Not much chance of him being found, though, out in the outer deeps."

Gaunt laughed shortly. "There'd have been no need for any of it if you'd arrived up to time. Where in hell have you been all this time? You were due three days ago."

"We've been having trouble with the stem rocket tubes. This tub isn't good for many more trips, chief. We've patched them up, but I don't like the look of 'em even now. Sooner we clear the gravity fields of the big fellows, the better I'll like it."

"Plenty of stuff aboard?"

"Say, there's enough platinum here to make us all millionaires for life. All those little trades we've done will be fleabites compared to this lot. Wait till you see it!"

"That's just what I am waiting for!" Gaunt retorted. "And step on it, will you? I can't leave here until you come: there's no other ship, remember."

"OK. Be with you in twenty-four hours...."

"Right." Gaunt switched off, slowly rubbed his hands together in anticipation. Illicit platinum mining on Io was distinctly profitable, and well worth the risk.

With a daredevil like Gates to do the work, and this lonely outpost as a distributing station to the shady buyers of various colonized planets.... Easy! Wonderfully easy! Probably Curt Vernol was better dead, after all. Had he only gone into space to finish his time, he might have learned too much....

"Far better dead," Gaunt murmured reflectively—then he frowned in surprise as the normal Earth radio wave started the signalling apparatus off again. Puzzled, he tuned in.

"Chief Earth Observatory calling Observatory Ten," came the recorded message. "You will take full details of star known as Acron 3784, between the paths of Canopus and Delta Argus, almost at the entrance of the Great Cleft in Argus. This star, which is probably of the temporary order, came into being as a fourth-magnitude star. Has now dropped to the fifth magnitude. Report in detail and give reasons. Earth observations none too clear. That is all. Please acknowledge receipt of these instructions,"

"Message received. Acron 3784 will be investigated by Observatory Ten," Gaunt transmitted, and switched off.

## Chapter 2: Acron 3764

The matter was purely routine work. Stars that come and go are common enough. Gaunt got to his feet and strode to the vast high-powered telescope in the centre of the great room, and swung round the pilot telescope, until at last Acron was on the line-divided finder. Moving to the controlling panel, he soon had the star centered exactly on the great viewing mirror of mercuroid alloy. The reflector, utilizing new magnetic means of trapping light waves, produced an image that was flawless and still.

Gaunt dimmed the lights, studied the image carefully. Acron had always been a bit of a mystery, anyway—one of that strange family of mystically born stars which make their sudden appearance in various parts of the sky, and then probably vanish just as strangely.

Fourth magnitude to fifth? Gaunt turned away from the screen and got to work with his spectroheliograph, made the usual routine study. The star was a main-sequence star of the G-type, and of typical solar characteristics. The spectrum of its photosphere was crossed by innumerable fine dark lines produced by the metallic absorptions in its higher atmosphere, together with definite evidences of calcium. Mass was almost identical with Earth's sun. Acron 3784 was indeed pretty similar to thousands of other main sequence stars in the universe, save in the matter of its sudden drop in magnitude.

Gaunt yawned a little. So what? He had checked

up, and that was all there was to it. Thoughtfully, he went on checking the absolute magnitude a star of that type could stand. It had dropped from magnitude 4.7 to exactly 5.53, and was still dropping....

Gaunt stroked his chin. That lay pretty close to instability. Anything below 6.78 magnitude would pass the star over the borderline from main sequence type to white dwarf....

He turned back to the screen. Other things were visible on Acron. Its brilliant photosphere, shielded by the telescope's dark glass screens, was punctured with rapidly growing spots—scars that spread visibly from the equatorial regions as the moments passed by. Definitely, the marks were sunspots, occurring at tremendous speed. Gaunt remembered the phenomenon was by no means uncommon. He had seen stars eat themselves out in this fashion in a matter of hours.

Pensive, he continued to watch. The change in magnitude was now explained.

The star was suffering from a severe attack of sunspots, spreading where no normal sunspots should, from equator to poles. As the minutes went by the magnitude dropped still more.

Gaunt's last reading was 5.82. He relayed that observation to Earth, promised further details as they came through, then turned to the more important matter of watching space for some sign of Ranvil Gates. But the telescope only gave a view of the eternal stars. As yet, Gates' ship was not in sight.

Gaunt thought of Curt Vernol's shattered body far

out in the wastes. A cold smile touched his lips.... He turned the reflector back to Acron....

Acron had changed again. Its face was a mass of spots; many of them obviously thousands of miles wide. Its light too had dimmed considerably.

Again Gaunt calculated....

Magnitude 6.80. The star was over the stability region. In that case— Gaunt shrugged. Just another stellar death, taking place at such a speed it could be viewed at leisure. Not that Gaunt wanted to view it, anyway: he had other things to worry him.

Once more he turned to the radio and gave his final report that Acron 3784 had crossed the stability line and would descend rapidly to a white dwarf state and finally expire altogether. Then he turned from the apparatus and glanced at his watch. He had time to get a sleep, and by then Gates should be somewhere close at hand.

He left the reflector mechanism in operation, slowly turning to follow Acron. No sense in setting the thing twice: he'd have to make one more general analysis report, anyhow.

\* \* \* \* \* \* \*

Gaunt awoke suddenly, aware that for some time his incoherent dreaming had been disturbed by a curious sound—a far distant hissing sound that was totally alien to the usually sepulchral quiet of this lone world. Normally, there was not a single sound save for the solemn snicking of the electric clocks.

Gaunt thought of Gates, of the dead Curt Vernol, of Acron 3784. Then he got off the bed and looked through the thick glass of the window. There was nothing save the far distant, pinpoint sun and rugged, barren rock. No sign of Gates: no sign of anything.

Rubbing his tousled head he switched on the lights and shuffled into the observatory, yawning as he went. Then his yawn stopped halfway as he crossed the threshold of the doorway. He stared blankly, utterly unable to comprehend what he saw.

In the centre of the huge place, where he had left the great reflector to follow Acron, was a hole. No reflector was present: the glass roof yawned like an empty eye. And on the metal floor was that hole, perfectly circular, buzzing and hissing like a hive of bees, filled within its expanse with deep, deadly black—the coal black of space that spoke of total absence of light reflection.

Gaunt gave a huge gulp and became suddenly aware that his knees were shaking with shock at the incredible thing that had come to pass. With baffled eyes he went closer to the hole and stared at it. It was perhaps two feet deep in the immensely tough metal floor, faultlessly shorn round the edges and growing wider and wider as he stared at it.

At last his gaze rose to the massive pillars that had supported the reflector. They were chopped off clean, as though with a vast blade. In an exact line from the glass in the roof to the hole in the floor, covering a width of two feet, everything solid had totally disappeared! The reflector bearings, the screen, the cables....

All the lot.

Eighty tons of solid metal gone in five hours or so? Metal flooring too, that was made to withstand the ravages of space cold? Even virgin basic rock on which the Observatory was built? Gaunt licked his suddenly dry lips, stared over the hole toward the radio apparatus.... So far that was untouched.

Then as the buzzing went on without interruption, he looked round him again. The bearings of the vanished reflector were still disappearing into thin air, working slowly downward toward him. And that hole in the floor was increasing....

He turned suddenly, reached behind him and took up a metal rod from the workbench. Tentatively, he waved it above the hole. Nothing happened. Then he dropped it right into the hole. The buzzing seemed to become transiently louder, then the rod vanished utterly.

Gaunt frowned deeply. His fear had gone for the moment: instead, the scientist in him was uppermost. This thing had to have an explanation, and the root of that explanation seemed to be Acron 3784. He turned swiftly to the main window and stared out onto the deeps at the spot where Acron should have been. But it was no longer visible—not to the naked eye, at least. Like thousands of other temporary stars Acron had disappeared entirely.

"It had to vanish, anyway," Gaunt muttered. "Once it crossed the stability line it was bound to become a white dwarf. First it had sunspots, which abnormally reduced its radiation. It crossed the line of safety

SOMETHING FROM MERCURY | 63

and started to contract at terrific speed. The more it contracted, the more the internal temperature rose and the more the surface cooled. The internal temperature would destroy the atoms in Acron's interior: there'd just be free electrons and stripped nuclei. Rapidly, the effect spread to the photosphere and that too collapsed. Acron became a white dwarf of densely packed material in an incredibly short space of time.... And what happened when that contractive process began?"

He mused for a moment, went on talking to the air.

"Obviously, the destruction of the atoms and the vast electronic changes would release radiation through space. Thousands of years of normal supply would be squandered in an instant. No more atoms to dam back the flood, no anything except a sudden outflow of all sorts of radiation. Then the white dwarf stage...."

"Radiation," he repeated softly, turning to look back at the hole. "Radiation was concentrated right there. That telescope being of magnetic light wave-trapping qualities, would draw both light waves and all other radiations to a focus, conduct them down the tubes onto the mercuroid mirror. Whatever radiations were given off by Acron at the moment of its final collapse were concentrated here. And then...."

Gaunt stopped suddenly, moved to his instrument rack, and took down a delicately balanced electrical apparatus. It was a Briggs Electronic Detector, so called by reason of its delicately balanced ability to check up on the vibrations of individual electrons in any given matter or gas. Carefully he fixed the highly complex controls and studied the testing screen keenly.

Thirty minutes passed.... An hour. And the hole had grown larger. When Gaunt finally studied his readings he could hardly credit his eyes.

"Is it possible?" he muttered. "Nothing but electrons in that hole. Negative electrons. No protons whatever: no opposite electric charge. One charge without the other, therefore nothing. For some reason protons have cancelled out and all that remains is.... Is the primal constituent of the universe. Negative electrons."

He became silent, turning the thing over in his mind. The buzzing worried him, so did the gradually expanding hole and vanishing metal pillars.... But the scientific riddle had stirred him. Slowly he went across to his desk and drew paper and pencil to him, began to figure slowly and thoughtfully, regardless of everything save the mystery that confronted him.

When at last he became conscious of his surroundings again, he had the thing clear. It was remarkable enough, but the only possible solution.

"So I've stumbled on it," he breathed, staring in front of him. "The secret of space and matter! Some early scientists believed that there might be two classes of electricity in the universe with definite opposite effects, but found only one, which they called 'neutral,' though its effects were either positive or negative according to the balance achieved. Their investigations showed us that the blasting away of atoms at the moment of a star slipping into the white dwarf stage left only uncontrolled negative electrons which radiated an energy that can only be classed as negative energy. Negative energy then, is space itself. That negative energy is backed by the whole preponderance of space. It was conducted down the mirror tubes and set up a negative energy field of terrific power, which overbalanced and cancelled the power of the positive protons, destroying the atoms themselves and leaving only electrons. And, since that original field was backed by all the vast preponderance of space, as against only the small positive units constituting the planet and all it contained, positive and negative do not balance any more. There is only negative—expanding space—in the hole!"

Gaunt looked back at his computations, surveyed them absently.

"That makes it clear," he murmured. "It makes clear why there are such enormous ranges of empty space compared to the amount of solid matter therein. Only on rare occasions does the positive field balance the negative, and then matter comes into being. Space—negative energy—is the dominant factor. It explains why the stars are surrounded by millions of miles of emptiness....

"Unintentionally, I have solved the whole secret of the universe. In the beginning there was only negative. From somewhere there came drifting positive fields, maybe from an extra-universal source, and so matter was born wherever the fields crossed and balanced. And now...."

## Chapter 3: The Growing Circle of Death

Gaunt rose to his feet. The obvious thing to do was to communicate his discovery to Earth. He had discovered something that scientists had tried to find for generations—the answer to the mystery of which came first—space or matter?'

He swung toward the radio apparatus—then stopped dead. It had become encompassed in the area of that vastly swollen hole. The vital wires to the generators had gone into nothing. The whole floor around it yawned in a deepening, utterly black pit. Communication with Earth, with anywhere for that matter, was definitely finished.

For the first time, Gaunt felt a vague qualm of fear. Up to now he had been absorbed in the interest of his discovery—but it was suddenly forced upon him that whatever he knew was entirely his own knowledge. He could not pass it on. Further, he was on a shrinking world, fast transforming itself into primal space-stuff.

He tried to think coherently, glanced quickly at the clock. The lapse of time during his deductions amazed him. Ranvil Gates ought to be somewhere in sight now. Upon him relied the only chance of getting off this collapsing world.

Gaunt leapt to the window and stared out at the stars. There was no sign of a distant glittering speck, no hint whatever of Gates being anywhere near.... He drummed his fingers agitatedly on the window frame, looked back at the; widening hole. Before very long it would have encompassed the entire laboratory floor, and since it went downward at unknown, but great, speed it would only be a matter of hours before it pierced clean through this small world and allowed the deadly cold of space to sweep through. The entire little globe would be like an apple with a hole bored through it.

"No!" Gaunt whispered. "No! I won't be trapped here! Gates will come! He's got to come!"

He turned nervously and snatched his spacesuit from its cupboard. Hastily he clambered into it. He took one last look at the relentless hole, then tore open the three airlocks and went blundering outside onto the ragged plain....

The stars winked down at him steadily. He fancied he must have been a victim of hysteria for a moment or two. He lost awareness of his immediate surroundings, came back to himself with the realization that he had travelled some distance from the observatory and had now brought up sharp with his back against frowning black rock. His legs were shaking oddly. Perspiration poured down his face inside his stifling suit. He gazed wildly up at the stars.

And suddenly he saw something. A faint, not very far distant glimmer. He was practised enough in space lore to recognize the object as a lone space flyer. His heart gave a mighty leap. The object was coming nearer, beyond doubt, backed by distant, sullen Jupiter and the giant worlds.

"Gates!" Gaunt screamed, inside his helmet. "Gates!

I knew you'd come! Thank God! Thank God!"

He turned and scrambled up the low rim of rock behind him, gradually blundered to the top—stood a lone figure silhouetted against the stars. He waved his arms frantically, watched with an insane desperation as the glittering speck came nearer....

At last it was no longer a speck but a visibly cigar-shaped object. It was perhaps a hundred miles away now, perfectly distinct in the airless vacuum,

Again Gaunt waved his bloated arms, but the flyer showed no signs of coming toward him....

He stared at it hungrily, then with a feeling of sickly horror as he saw it was only three-quarters of a ship The back half had been blown away by some force or other, blown away so completely that there was not even the derelict section trailing behind, chained by mass.

The stern rocket tubes! Suddenly Gaunt remembered Gates' message: They had been giving trouble, and if seized up— They *had* seized up! Gaunt knew enough of space flying to recognize the trouble. The explosive gases had not passed off freely, but instead had smashed the jet tubes and blown out the back part of the ship. And in that old pirate tub there were no safety compartments, even granting there had been time to use them. So far as Gaunt could judge, the ship's occupants must have died instantly from the sudden inrush of vacuum.

The ship was now just drifting along with its original momentum, too far away from the planet to actually reach it. The counteractive fields of the giant planets were too great. In the end it would probably halt, then drift slowly. back toward the orbits of Pluto and Neptune....

Gaunt realized all these things with a deep inner numbness. A hundred miles or so between him and a life of constant luxury. Had he only been able to reach the ship, space-suited as he was, he would have found some way to patch it up until he reached friends on other planets. All he could do now was watch the ship drift slowly away, until at last it vanished in the blaze of the stars....

A deep sigh escaped him. He cursed the regulation that did not permit a man to have a spare spaceship; that forced him to wait until he was freed by the ship of the relief man.

Little by little he realized his last chance had gone. He was alone on this world. Gates was dead; the radio was useless; no regular ships came out this far. The whole vast vault of infinity was empty of craft. Only the stars—the everlasting stars.

He had solved the secret of the universe, had seen a fortune and escape drift by under his nose, and now—

He swung round suddenly. Out of the tail of his eye he saw something happen to the observatory. Staring at it, he saw it quickly cave inward with all four walls—collapse into a vast black circle that matched the dark of space....

He sat down shakily, felt curiously light-headed. He knew the reason immediately. One cause was his intense emotion, and the other was the slow lessening of gravitation. As the mass of the planet was slowly converted into space, the gravity correspondingly lowered. He was losing weight.

Turmoiled thoughts whirled through his brain. Stranded on a world all by himself—the victim of malign circumstances. There had to be a way to escape this crumbling prison! He had done nothing to deserve death, anyway. Besides—

Nothing to deserve it? Suddenly he recalled Curt Vernol, and with the recollection came a vast wave of bitter self-reproach. He did not regret slaying Vernol—he'd been too inquisitive anyway—but he did curse himself for a fool for having fired him away into the void in his ship. He had thrown away his one means of escape....

Thrown away everything!

Dazedly, he stared at the hole. It was expanding with terrific speed. The small hills ringed it round. It was advancing inexorably toward him. Before long the planetoid itself would crack in half.

Death was inevitable. Gaunt realized it now—but *death*, when he had expected so much! He fancied he could hear Curt Vernol laughing at him. Perhaps his spirit still pervaded this crumbling world—

Gaunt shook himself. This was pure fancy. Things had gone against him, yes, but in a perfectly logical fashion. But that did not make matters any better.

Suddenly he was calm again, faced the situation. He had done wrong: he realized it now. But he was still a scientist, and he still had the courage that had led him to take this lonely job and at the same time defy interplanetary laws. Even if his private aims had collapsed, even if he had committed cold-blooded murder, he still loved the profession that was closest to his heart.

Mastering himself, he tugged a safety cylinder from his belt, removed the curved plate from within it and started to work with the stylus. There was no reason why science should not know of the thing he had discovered. Someday, perhaps, the cylinder would be picked up—granting it missed being annihilated when the planetoid collapsed.

At last he had finished his message, packed it carefully into the cylinder, then fired the small rocket attached to it. In grim immovability he watched it soar away into the darkness above him.

He looked back at the hole, smiled twistedly. At any moment now the whole planetoid would break in pieces.

Slowly he got to his feet, slid down the black rocks, walked steadily toward that abysmal circle.

The eternal stars watched him go.

# PRE-NATAL

Seated in this vast, cool room, this Library of the Intellectuals as it is called—gazing out through the broad window now and again upon sweeping, park-like spaces broken only by slender buildings reaching to the serene blue sky, I am conscious in some measure of the amazing thing which has happened to me.

For all this is so different from Earth. I suppose it should give me a feeling of desolation to realize that I have left Earth forever, severed all human connection with it—yet no such emotion is upon me.

Indeed, it is in an effort to analyse exactly how I do feel that I am writing these words, in the hope that memory will recall the events in a more ordered sequence. Later I shall dispatch this document into space in the hope that somebody—if I set the mechanism aright—will find it upon the Earth. It may clear up a good deal that is puzzling.

So then, to my story—

About a year after I had settled to agricultural work about twenty miles south of Michigan, and had generally got things running very satisfactorily, curious occurrences began to attract my attention, and for that matter the attention of the whole of the United States in that mellow late summer of 2014.

There were lights in the sky over Michigan State. Anyway, the lights were extraordinary—nor for that matter were they entirely confined to Michigan, for other cities reported them also. But always they were seen over one or the other city, and never over a whole number of cities at once.

In appearance they were rather like nebulous, great, hazy balls at an indeterminable height. Wherever they occupied a space filled normally by stars, the stars had to surrender their glory to the new presence.

At first the weather and air authorities were the only people interested. They worked in co-operation and sent up stratosphere pilots to investigate. These men went to the absolute limit of ceiling, and returned to report that the lights were as far off from the atmosphere limit as they were from earth's surface.

In truth the light fields must be an enormous distance off, and nothing but a spaceship could track them down. This being right out of the question, the puzzled authorities turned to the scientists—and particularly the astronomers, for suggestions.

Hardly had the scientists agreed to look into the matter before overzealous news editors immediately smeared their papers with headlines about gas-like visitors from other worlds. This view was strongly condemned by science a few days later, however, when it became apparent that these light fields were not detached, isolated masses of light floating in space but had a definite connection with somewhere beyond....

I wonder how I can make it clearer? It was, you see, as though we were looking into the remote end of a searchlight beam, and as long as the projection was dead in line with our vision, the 'end' looked like a floating light patch.... But after four days, when the lights had come back to Michigan, they had also shifted position slightly so that we could see the beams that projected them, beams that narrowed away into the infinite deeps of space, where unimaginable distance swallowed them completely.

They looked now like dagger-shaped bars in the sky, the broadest end nearest to us and the 'point' swallowed in distance. Considering the hugeness of stellar distances, it made my mind reel when I tried to picture how big they really were.

So, from the isolated position of my farmstead I had a good view of all this, and like the rest of the people in the country wondered what it was all about. Somehow I couldn't see them being invaders or even invaders' weapons. More likely some kind of cosmic 'fault.'

For over a week the lights remained over Michigan, then they showed signs if shifting about the sky again. I was watching their amazing movements in the starry sky—as though they were searchlights with no traceable source—when I was aware of footsteps coming up the hard cinder track leading to my farmhouse.

Turning, I peered into the gloom. To my surprise I realized it was Charlie Ellis—but to find his thickset figure and square, good-humoured face beside me at this hour, for it was close on midnight, was definitely unusual.

Charlie, you see, was an agricultural research chemist, engaged on Government work, ferreting out details on phosphates, fertilizers, and so on. It was because of his occupation that we had come to know each other so well. In fact, I'm willing to admit that half my success was due to his advice.

"Pretty, aren't they?" he said, locking his hands behind him and appraising the heavens. Then he added in a sombre voice, "If they were only pretty I wouldn't be worried...."

I took my eyes from their vague, apparently aimless, searching to stare at Charlie's upturned face. It was grimmer than I had ever seen it.

"Why, what do you mean?" I asked him.

"They're dangerous, Bob. I happen to know because I spend my time amongst scientists—so I'm in a position to hear things that are barred from the general public. That's the reason I'm here now. You'd be well advised to quit this spot for as long as the lights remain."

"Quit!" I stared at him. "But that's ridiculous! Besides, quitting is about the last thing a man of the land can do. Nature just won't be monkeyed with."

"If your life is more valuable than Nature, you'll quit!" He lowered his eyes to look at me, then jerked his head towards the farmhouse. "Come on in and I'll tell you what I know...."

So over coffee and sandwiches, he started in to explain.

"Those lights," he said, "are ultra-cosmic. And to give them their proper name—the name given to them by the Science Bureau, anyway—they're life probes."

I frowned at him.

"Life probes," he repeated. "That's a fanciful term for them, I suppose, but it's quite near the truth. As you know, stratosphere pilots and even spatial observers have never been able to get anywhere near them, but instruments down at the Bureau have analysed what they have filmed and recorded, and measured their intensity, depth, composition—everything about them. The sum total of these tests is that they are fatal to life as we know it. Were we to duplicate their qualities—which we could quite easily—everything living, human, animal, or vegetable would be utterly destroyed."

"Then it's electricity or some kind of radiation?" I hazarded.

"In a sense—but it would be more correct to say it is a sort of force. Where it has been generated, what its purpose is, no man knows. But the fact remains that should one of those rays come right down to Earth here, it would be goodbye to everything and everybody within a ten-mile radius."

I smiled at Charlie incredulously. His face lost none of its grimness.

"I'm not telling you any of this for the fun of it, Bob. It's cast-iron truth, every bit of it."

"Even supposing it is," I argued, "what reason have you for assuming that any of them will come down to earth here, of all places?"

"The best reason in the world! They've been searching now for long enough—everybody knows that—and finally they seem to have made up their minds to settle over Michigan. Even so, though this State is their main area, they don't stay put. They're still looking for something. Any hour, any minute, they may find what they're looking for.... If they do, God help the people any of those lights settle upon!"

"But whom do you mean by 'they'?" I demanded. "Are you suggesting that men of some kind, living beings, are connected with all this?"

"Intelligent minds of some sort, yes. Either they are located on some far-off planet, or else in another Universe altogether. That we don't know." Charlie stopped and clenched his fist. "I know one thing, Bob—if it were left to me I'd have every city where the lights are hovering evacuated."

I was silent for a long time, thinking it over, then I shrugged.

"You can make it sound pretty ominous, Charlie."

"I'm only giving you the views of the scientists. And it struck me that you being alone here, far from the nearest town, might make you a far more vulnerable target than if you were one of millions in a city. If those things descend to Earth anywhere near here, you'd be killed, sure as eggs."

"But they mightn't," I pointed out, rather dryly. "Anyway, I can't go and pull things to bits just because of a notion like this. I appreciate your motives, of course, only—"

"All right, all right." He got to his feet, a trifle huffed. "It's entirely up to you. Maybe I'm wrong: I surely hope so."

I saw him to the door. For a moment we both stood looking up at the shifting lights, then with a nod of farewell he left me. For a long time I remained surveying that odd sky, wondering what it was all about; then I turned back into the house and in a thoughtful mood prepared for bed.

I could not have been asleep for more than a couple of hours when I was awakened by the most curious, rushing noise. Oddly enough, I had been dreaming I was skiing and had suddenly been caught in an avalanche—so I had a little difficulty in sorting out reality from fancy. Certainly the noise that now gushed upon me was exactly similar to the sliding of great masses of snow down a long, smooth roof.

Instantly I was out of bed, considerably startled. The house, the whole farm in fact, was alive with noise. The dogs out in the yard were barking furiously—

The noise increased suddenly even as I staggered across to the window to see what was wrong. There burst upon me the most unforgettable sight. The vision of the countryside saturated in trembling, quivering light—intense white light—as far as I could see.

I had little time to study the matter, but it did strike me that my farm was in the very centre of the glare, for as I ran from window to window, thereby encompassing all points, I was greeted with this same blinding vision.

Quivering, in a sudden dread of expectancy, I waited. All Charlie Ellis' grim warnings came tumbling back into my mind now. He had said that nothing could live if one of the lights dropped down to Earth— Yet here I was, fully alive, in the midst of one!

Or *was* I fully alive? I attempted an analysis of myself. I was trembling like the devil and a curious weakness was stealing over me. It was an appalling sensation. I can only say it felt as though I were being literally lifted out of myself, as though my mind were being taken apart from my body.

Upon my ears came a sudden chorus of sounds—the furious barking of the dogs, the neighing of disturbed horses in the distant stables, even the mad screech of a pig. Then something seemed to jerk me and I was seized with unbearable tension. I reeled dizzily—

Then for perhaps five seconds I was treated to the astounding sight of beholding my own body! There it lay on the floor, hastily dressed in pants, shirt, and slippers. The dead, glassy eyes stared up at me.

Brief indeed was the vision. I had no time to assimilate it before a vast wave of darkness overwhelmed me. I was flying into an abyss...somewhere.

Yes, I was somewhere; it was not a sudden awareness of the fact, but rather a gradual realization like the slow awakening from a deep and pleasant slumber. I lay perfectly still, staring up at a multitude of stars. Never had I seen so many. They spawned in myriad curtains wherever I turned my gaze....

I suppose I had a body. I say this because I could not see one—yet all the appropriate actions were apparently there. I .am since inclined to think it was some kind of mental body I possessed rather than the flesh and blood variety.

So I got to my feet and looked about me. I have already mentioned the stars.... As for the rest of my environment, it was made up of a vast rocky plain receding into distance where it fell into the backdrop of harshly glittering gems.

Rocks—rocks—rocks. Everywhere! And at my feet a hard merciless ground without a spark of life. Where was I? How in God's name had I ever gotten into this? It was not Earth; it was not a place I had ever known before.

I was aware of something else too, the swishing and straining of a myriad thoughts. Not my own, but vast, incomprehensible thoughts seeming to swirl in a sea all around me, and as though I were a living island. Standing here trying to imagine what had happened, I felt the breath of genius. Superhuman genius.

At last some impulse stirred me forward. Here I got a surprise. I did not walk. I simply travelled over the surface of the ground as lightly as thistledown. Indeed, I am hard put to explain my circumstances. So far as I could tell then, I was possessed of an extra-mundane body and lost on a planet, which had neither air nor life, and which was situated God knew where.

Travelling as I did, I covered distances at tremendous speeds, and shortly found that I had been wrong in my assumption concerning the planet's lifelessness. There *was* life of the vegetable kind, for I was halted now before a jungle of fantastic, nightmarish outlines. It looked utterly impassable—a vast, twisted wilderness of massive trees, interlocked branches, solid curtains of vines and undergrowth. And all of it was indescribably sinuous and malignant, the embodiment of evil design.

I stood looking at it from a rock, perplexed, for it completely barred my path, nor could I rise sufficiently to travel over the top of it. Then somebody was beside me. I did not see him nor could I hear him in this airless void. But he was there.

"Who—who are you?" I asked, but no words escaped me. It was a purely mental question. Likewise the reply was mental, and very astonishing it was.

"I am to be your constant companion from now on. I have always been with you in life, though you may not have been aware of it. I am your shield in moments of extreme danger," There was a little pause, then: "I am Self-Preservation."

This stunned me for a moment, then I protested.

"This is absurd! You are another being, as I am."

"No, I am a part of you. A living thing is born of mind. All the attributes of mind—fear, self-preservation, lust, ambition, and so on—exist as separate emotional waves—like those of the electron—to be destroyed or accepted according to desire. You understand?"

"No," I responded, struggling to understand the

overwhelming dream-like state of everything.

"Anyway," came the thought, after a pause, "I shall be with you, advising you, directing you. Not always will you sense my thoughts: you will act apparently of your own volition. But it will be my power back of you...."

"What *happened*?" I asked. "I'm confused. Did I die?"

"Your flesh and blood framework died, yes, but that was only a useless, clumsy carcase. It is the mental life which counts."

"This, then, is beyond death?"

"No, this is before birth!"

Silently I wrestled with the impossible. He—or it—must have sensed it, for after a while he communicated again.

"You have a long, hard journey ahead of you, but I shall be ready to help you.... That jungle there: do you know what it is?"

As I remained silent, he finished, "It is the Jungle of Evil. You must find your way through it, with my help."

Again came the impulse to start forward, then I was arrested by a thunderous thought wave. I can only liken it to a mighty voice, like the Voice of the Abyss itself.

"He will live! He must live! A greater, better man than any we have ever known...."

"What—what was that" I questioned, startled.

"The Voice of Science," came the ambiguous response. "You may hear it often, during the journey....

But come, we have much to vanquish...."

As the thunderous notes of that mental voice died out, we went on again, drifting as before over rocky ground. With a disconcerting swiftness the labyrinth of the Jungle of Evil loomed upon us. I hesitated for just a moment, appalled by its tangled, merciless density.

Like everything else in this incredible land, it was at variance with all the laws of Nature. It was not vegetable life, as I had at first thought, but something beyond analysis—rubbery, twisted, malign. Again I was tempted to wonder if it were more a manifestation of thought than aught else....

Then Self-Preservation communicated. "Advance! I shall be with you."

The demand on my courage was enormous, but I obeyed and glided into the midst of the tangle. Immediately the queer trees lashed in deadly fury, trying to bar my path. And here was the strange thing. The barrier they formed was mental, not physical, for with my extra-mundane body I could easily have passed through their midst.

Instead I was harassed, overwhelmed indeed, by a succession of mental onslaughts which all but finished me. As the trees and vines moved to grasp me, I sensed emotions I had once known on Earth—jealousy, hatred, vindictiveness, lust—all the baser emotions. Against these I was compelled to fight with every scrap of my mental power, and as I fought, one after the other of the branches and vines fell away from me and I pushed on deeper into the jungle. Somewhere, I presumed, Self-

Preservation was with me, for I felt convinced I could never have made this fight alone.

So at last, as I progressed, the jungle began to thin, and the strangling, battering emotions dropped away from me. I came to a clearing at length, filled with a surging joy at discovering the jungle was behind. Even so, the view ahead was none too encouraging.

There was a sea ahead—sapphire blue. Or rather there was a bay. It looked deceptively calm with its lazy wavelets dropping softly on the rocky shingle. Beyond it, about two miles I judged, reared mountains. They seemed to go up for miles, climbing to the blazing stars.

Standing here, or at least poised here, I was swept for a moment by a terrible loneliness, a consciousness of the mad, bizarre nature of my adventure. Was I dead or alive? Man or Spirit? Still I did not know, but I imagined a lost soul in Limbo would feel pretty much as I did.

Then again that awful smashing thought wave—the Voice of Science—battered into me.

"There can be no doubt that this is the perfect man! With each probe of our instruments more of the distracting heritages are purged. Unquestionably we shall finally produce a pure, purged mind-force.... And with it—life! We must stir this inanimate clay into existence. We must!"

What was he, or it, talking about? As if in answer, I felt Self-Preservation contacting me again.

"That was the Voice of Science again. Before you

can know what it really means, you have the final barriers to cross. There they are—ahead of you. The Sea of Heredity and the Mountains of Birth. Can you but cross the one and scale the other, you will be born."

"Will it be dangerous?" I questioned.

"Very! On whether you succeed or not depends your chance of being born. If you fail, then you will remain forever as just a thought, incapable of physical expression."

I pondered over this for a moment, then advanced to the ocean's edge and stared at it. Strange, imponderable shapes moved inside the sapphire. Mirror-like, crystal clear, I saw my parents smiling up at me gravely, then my grandparents with less distinctness—and so on right down the scale of my ancestry until it dissolved in a common blur of antiquity.

"The Sea of Heredity," Self-Preservation reminded me. "Conquer this and you purge yourself of all ancestral influences. If there were ever disease, or emotional excesses, or anything like that in your heritage, now is your time to destroy them. Mentally, not physically, for as you must realize by now the physical is but a reflection of the mental. So—proceed. I shall be with you."

Again I had to nerve myself. I had imagined I would be able to float over this savagely blue sea, as I had over the land—but no such concession was granted me. The moment I reached its edge, I felt myself drawn irresistibly into its depths—literally tugged down until I was smothering.

As it had been in the Jungle of Evil, so again now I

was swept with convictions of inherited tendencies—a quickness of temper, a tendency to cancer, and a myriad little foibles that had suddenly become real, vital things.

I fought them desperately, and the harder I fought, the more I seemed to progress and the less potent they became.... Then at last, when I felt I should have to give up from sheer mental exhaustion, I became aware that the all-encompassing blue darkness had gone.

I was on solid rock again at the base of the mountain range and the sea was behind me.

"You conquered!" I sensed Self-Preservation was with me again.

"And now?" I questioned, realizing that my mind was becoming surprisingly clear and freed from all former human drawbacks.

"Now for the ascent to Birth! It will be hard, painful, as your mind becomes clothed in a physical body. But you will triumph, have no fear."

I turned to the foothills, paused for a moment to stare at those vast and jagged peaks. Then I began to climb. Immediately it was as if I were borne up towards the stars. It was a terrifying sensation, almost like falling upward into the sky....

As I went up the stars resolved into a welling blur of light. Pains shot through me for the first time since my adventure had begun. New sounds reached me which I heard, no longer sensing them by telepathy.

Slowly, very slowly, I became aware of the fact that I had a body, legs, arms, trunk, head.... I opened my eyes abruptly to stare into serious, puzzled faces. There were six men around me, garbed in white and masked to the eyes.

Surgeons!

One of them spoke, and I recognized the Voice of Science.

"Where—where am I?" I whispered—and it struck me as odd that I wasn't speaking English; yet the language seemed habitually familiar to me.

The man did not answer the question but he glanced at the others with triumph in his eyes.

"He lives!" he cried. "Our reasoning was correct! We moulded the common chemical elements of a man, and then set out to probe the wastes of space to find a mind which could give him life...."

"Once," I said, "I was a man of Earth. You killed me!"

The leading surgeon turned, looked at me sharply.

"Explain!" he commanded.

So I did, and at the end of it he nodded thoughtfully.

"Earth, as you call it, is to us but an infinitesimal speck somewhere in a microcosmic universe—somewhere in that globe there—" And he nodded to a device supported between mighty power magnets. "Universes within universes, and ours the greater."

I stared at the globe with its lambent fires. Earth—the whole Earthly Universe indeed—there? God!

"Throughout space," the surgeon resumed, "there flows eternal thought energy. We here had to capture a single unit of that energy and so we set our absorber rays to the task. One point, we found, was excessively rich in thought energy. That point was probably the Earth you speak of. Even finer focuses narrowed down at last to a single thought-unit—you! Isolated from others.... It was pure luck we happened to find you."

"The remainder? Your story of Self-Preservation, the Sea of Heredity, and so on? Purely the mental aspects occasioned by your journey to the point where you took over the body. Our instruments deliberately purged your thought-unit of all hereditary and evil instincts because we needed—and got—a pure, free mind to motivate this synthetic man. The first we have ever made which lives...."

"And the Voice of Science? My own—audible to you as you gradually came to the point of conscious life."

I looked down at myself. I was born again, shorn of all human anxieties and traits. Parentless, my mind purged. Slowly I began to smile as I looked at the scientists.

They smiled back at me, conscious of the immensity of their vast achievement....

# BEYOND ZERO

For the sake of convenience, Clayton Brook called himself a scientific engineer, which designation covered a multitude of activities, all of them more or less related to electronics, physics, and suchlike. The trouble with Clayton Brook was that he disliked concentration, otherwise he could no doubt have become one of the most brilliant scientists of all time.... As it was, he just drifted around, never staying very long in one occupation before he was eager to roam again.

Then came the scare of Atomic War, and Clayton, like many other scientists, was seconded to secret military research.

Eventually, however, the Atomic War scare had ended and the world drew back from the brink. He had been released to pursue his own activities, and was kicking around with no fixed idea of how to plan his future when he accidentally fell in again with Nick Farrish. During their government secondment in Electronics, the two had encountered each other quite a deal, usually in the maintenance centres, and it had been at such times as these that Nick had spoken of some 'terrific idea' which he had been intending to develop when 'demobbed.'

Well, release had come—and the chance meeting inevitably brought up the subject of the 'terrific idea' once again. Nick promptly invited Clayton Brook down to his home a quite unpretentious and pretty isolated place bordering the Sussex Downs. And it was here that the 'terrific idea' began to take shape—in words to commence with.

"I hardly need to tell you, Clay, that I'm a scientist," Nick Farrish remarked, grinning, as he prowled thoughtfully up and down the small laboratory he had in the basement of the house. "You know all about that from working beside me during the war scare."

"Certainly you always seemed to know the answers when it came to electronics," Clay agreed.

Nick nodded absently, the eulogy lost upon him. He was a tall, still young man, with complete disregard for his appearance, and having the sharp yet curiously faraway look in his grey eyes, which bespoke the scientist and the dreamer.

"I've been thinking—for years as a matter of fact—that there is one thing science has not yet conquered. I don't mean perpetual motion, or any of those things. I mean the Absolute Zero."

Clay looked surprised. "They've very nearly got as low as possible to minus 273 Centigrade anyhow! Just a fraction above it...."

"A fraction." Nick replied slowly. "That nonetheless makes all the difference in the world, or even the universe. It is assumed that as long as molecules move, there is heat-conversion: something is moving. But when movement entirely ceases, the absolute zero of temperature has been reached and molecular activity ceases."

"Which," Clay remarked. "is merely another way of outlining how the universe will eventually look when thermodynamics have done their stuff and the total energy of the universe is uniformly distributed at the same temperature."

"Well, yes, but that isn't quite what I mean. What I want to find out—in fact, what every scientist wants to find out—is what really happens when matter or any of its substance forms, like gas, air, and so forth, reach absolute zero. The total cessation of movement should, as I see it, mean no light, no heat, no time, no anything, except the displacement of a certain area of space in which the 'absoluted' substance is standing. In a word," he finished, looking at Clay pensively, "matter at total rest would be well worth any scientist's time to study."

"But how are you going to do it?" Clay demanded. "All the efforts of scientists have failed to produce the absolute. Do you think you can do better?"

Nick smiled. "Think I can? I *have*! I did it before I entered Electronics during the war scare, and after that I was so fully occupied in the Services I could go no further. I've begun to pick up the threads again, though, and all I have to do now is build the apparatus. I was just wondering about advertising for an assistant when we ran into each other. Call it coincidence, luck, or anything else you like, but there is no man I'd sooner have to help me than you. Besides, you're an engineer and a scientist and that's one hell of an advantage."

Clay hesitated. He was trying to overcome his surprise at the way in which Nick had stated he had accomplished a scientific miracle.

"I suppose." Clay said presently, "it will be an expensive experiment?"

"Fairly; but I know the best places to buy and I'm not exactly without money. My old man saw to that.... Look," Nick went on, "suppose you let *me* worry over the finance? Here is my proposition: if we can reach Absolute Zero between us, we can both get highly-paid technical posts in the physical laboratories for our trouble, and that's worth any scientist's effort. You've no particular employment at the moment, so...."

"All right." Clay interrupted, grinning. "I gather the drift. We do our best to achieve a scientific miracle, and then become super backroom boys for our trouble. All right with me. But put me out of my misery and tell me how you're going to create absolute zero."

Nick's answer to this was to produce a mass of plans and blueprints. Being an engineer, Clay understood what the blueprints were about, but when it came to the basic details he found himself floundering—and admitted the fact.

"First," Nick said, indicating the print, "we have this A-Z chamber, as I'll call it. It will be made of a copper-tungsten alloy. Through the axial-traps—directly facing each other on each side of the sphere—all the air will be withdrawn as in the usual process of creating a vacuum. That will still leave some molecules in motion, however, and therefore it won't be absolute zero. The last part we'll accomplish electromagnetically. Around the globe we have to set up electromagnetic stresses powerful enough to prevent the remaining molecules inside the globe from moving."

"In other words," Clay said, thinking, "you propose to use electrical energy to stop electrical energy? That will defeat its own purpose, Nick. The very fact of there being energy entering the vacuum will preclude absolute zero."

Nick was ready immediately with his answer. "No energy will actually enter the vacuum. I said 'stresses.' Electromagnetic fields of equal space-strain will operate on the outside of the A-Z chamber, exactly embracing the two hemispheres. Pulling in equal strength, they will halt the action of the molecules inside and suspend all movement, just as if they were at the dead centre of gravity. When that happens, the Absolute will have been achieved. This same dual-field of strain will prevent the Chamber itself from falling inwards through lack of resistance inside, and air pressure outside. The point is: motion, radiation, matter, or whatever else you like to name, will cease within the Chamber."

This, then, was how Nick Farrish put it—but the more Clay came to ponder upon it, and helped build the equipment, the more he realized the simplicity of the plan. All that Farrish was really doing was duplicating Nature's own law of gravitation—creating a warp in space, with the one difference that he was intending to use two warps of equal intensity, thereby 'freezing' the movement of whatever molecules lay between.

\* \* \* \* \* \* \*

It took two months to build the apparatus. The A-Z Chamber was eight feet in diameter, rather like a deep-sea bathysphere in appearance, cast in one complete piece with the exception of the small, three-foot-wide circles at opposite 'axial' ends through which the first ordinary 'vacuumising' was to be done. It was supported on a massive metal cradle rising two feet from the floor, and, planned with mathematical precision; the electromagnetic apparatus, composed of two massive bar magnets exactly opposite each other, were fixed into the floor at points facing each other. with the A-Z Chamber between them. The work of the switchboard was trifling once this major factor of the Chamber itself had been completed.

It was when the Chamber was finished that ideas occurred to Clay, and he promptly put them to Nick.

"This thing is going to be sealed up, Nick. How shall we know what's going on inside when the thing's opaque?"

"We shan't need to. Not during the process, anyway. First time out I shall simply try and reduce the empty vacuum itself to absolute zero, to see if it can be done. The meters on the switchboard will show whether or not we've been successful. If everything is okay, we'll use a bar of iron or something next time, iron being the basic matter of the universe. Then we'll see what it looks like after having touched absolute zero and been restored again."

"If there's anything to look at," Clay said, at which Nick gave a questioning glance.

"I mean." Clay added, "that when the motion of matter ceases there cannot be anything visible. All we see anyway is simply the extension of molecular speeds. When that speed slows to nothing, all trace must disappear, be it vegetable, animal, or mineral."

"I agree, but I said 'and restored again.' At absolute zero nothing can be visible because even light waves will have ceased their transmission—but restoration of the substance concerned should show us what changes the stuff has undergone in the process of reaching the absolute."

Clay nodded and thought it out. Finally he smothered a yawn and Nick glanced at his watch.

"Everything's done," he said, "and it's long past midnight. We'd better get some sleep. First thing tomorrow we'll try it out."

He smiled wistfully as he surveyed the equipment.

"I'd dearly love to try it out now, but I suppose it doesn't do to race the human machine too much. How I'm going to sleep with all this on my mind God alone knows."

Clay bade him goodnight and went up to the room he had been using whilst staying in the house. For a little while he sat thinking upon the marvel of the thing they were going to attempt, then with a sigh he felt for his cigarette case to have a last smoke before turning in. The case was missing. Frowning, Clay tried to think where he might have left it. Then it occurred to him that he must have dropped it inside the A-Z Chamber that evening when he had been making the finishing touches. He was of two minds whether to go after it or not; then he decided he had better do so in case it got overlooked when the experiment was made the following morning. Since it had a sentimental value, Clay had no wish to sec it reduced to absolute zero!

In three minutes Clay was back in the laboratory again. Evidently Nick had gone to bed, for the lights were out. Ignoring them, Clay switched on the extension-cable, which lighted the lamp inside the A-Z Chamber. Then he squirmed his way through the three-foot opening into the interior.

He began looking for his case and faded to see it, then in turning suddenly he caught his head on the swinging lamp and it extinguished itself with a broken filament.

"Blast!" Clay muttered.

It was pitchy dark inside the Chamber and he could only just see the round opening where he had climbed in. He felt around on the floor for his cigarette case and after a while detected its bard outline. It must have fallen edgewise against the curving wall and had escaped detection by reason of the walls being similarly polished.

At that moment, to Clay's surprise, the dim circular opening lighted suddenly behind him as the laboratory globes came up. Evidently Nick too had come back for something. Clay began to rise from his knees—and then gasped in amazement as the flex and extinguished lamp were suddenly withdrawn and the cap over the entrance-lock slammed shut.

Clay just could net credit it for a moment. He was in total, crushing darkness. What the devil was Nick playing at. anyway?

"Hey!" Clay yelled, pounding on the massively thick wall. "Hey, Nick! Let me out of here!"

Even as he pounded, Clay realized how useless it was. Nick could not hear him through the thick walls any more than Clay could hear movement in the laboratory. Then a frightening thought descended upon Clay. Had Nick come back into the laboratory for the express purpose of exhausting the A-Z Chamber to zero?

It would be just about like him! Possibly his restless temperament would not allow him to sleep, and he wanted to see what could be done with his idea instead of waiting for the morning. Inwardly Clay could not blame him. Nick had said he would dearly love to try out the invention there and then—and he could not know Clay was imprisoned in the Chamber because of the smashed light filament. He would accept the darkness of the Chamber as sufficient indication that it was quite empty....

Good God! Clay began to sweat profusely as he realized the horrible possibilities. He blundered around like a rat in a cage, banging against the curved, implacable

SOMETHING FROM MERCURY | 99

walls, yelling at the top of his voice, bewildered by the smothering, utter darkness. Then, though he could not hear anything, he did notice that the air was thinning! He could hardly draw breath.

Then Nick was reducing the Chamber to a vacuum! And after that...?

Clay's head swam as his lungs struggled desperately to inhale. Air was disappearing rapidly, and at length he fell to the polished floor, filled with the thundering conviction that he was about to die. In those few seconds he thought over everything he had ever done. His life reeled out before him like thread on an unspinning bobbin. Yet somehow he could not discover any specific incident which could account for an inscrutable destiny having placed him in a position like this.

He was no longer thinking coherently: that was it. For a while he even believed he must have been unconscious, but upon recovery from this condition, his mind remained acute even though he was quite unable to move any part of his body.

He was not conscious of breathing, or of his heart beating. All he did realize was the devouring darkness and a slow, creeping iciness affecting him. It increased by gradual degrees—a curious, frightening sensation of numbness. This, Clay was inclined to think, was the effect of the twin electromagnetic strains operating on the molecules of his body. Far back in his mind he realized that Nick had evidently decided to achieve Absolute Zero without waiting for the morning and—all unawares—he had made his best friend the subject!

Though Clay was not aware of his heart beating or of his lungs operating, he *did* feel the cold—a cold such as he had never experienced before—which followed the numbness. It had the searing, razor-edged keenness of interstellar space itself, biting beyond endurance...until it gradually began to give way before a conviction of drowsy pleasure. Clay felt relaxed and satiated, as though he had partaken of heavy meal and was at peace with the world.... At this same moment the darkness began to lift a trifle and he thrilled to the discovery that his eyes were still functioning anyway.

He expected to see the round hole in the A-Z Chamber and Nick's head and shoulders vignetted by it. But there was nothing like that. Instead, though Clay could not move, he could discern landscape. It grew clearer with the moments, merging out of indeterminate mist. He found with dawning amazement that he was looking at the South Downs surrounding the house and laboratory.

But they were unsteady and quivering! They shifted and moved as corn sways when the wind stirs it. From the house to the cliffs it was only half a mile's distance, and as he stared at these cliffs, beholding them immersed in the inexplicable metamorphosis of Change, Clay saw them curving and sagging inwards as if made of sand against which a flood tide was surging irresistibly.

It was only a vision, Clay told himself, but it suggested to him a most incredible thing. He was somehow moving in Time and at a terrific speed. What he had witnessed for a few brief moments—or had they been centuries?—had been sea erosion! He had seen the speeded-up process of that ponderously slow process measured normally by decades.

Then the cliffs and the sea were gone, dissolving into some new vision at which Clay stared intently. He was looking at a metallic spire, straight and shining as a needle piercing into a cobalt-blue sky. About it at a lower level other buildings melted slowly into view, inexpressibly graceful in outline. Clay saw vast colonnades of metal, plazas and terraces, trees and flowers of magnificent hue. The picture was suddenly acid-sharp.

Clay was lying on his back. Beneath him was grass so velvety in texture it felt like moss.

His first impulse was to move, but he could not. He was motionless—and astounded. He could not move his eyes, and it seemed to him that he did not blink either, yet he felt no sensation of discomfort through dust settling on his unprotected eyeballs.

Though the metallic spire was the main object at which he looked—the other details shading off as they spread beyond the line of vision—he was also aware of something curious in the cloudless blue sky. It was a golden band, a titanic mono-coloured rainbow arch, apparently motionless, starting from the horizon to the rear and at which Clay could not look, and ending at the horizon beyond the tall spire.

Where? Why? How? These were the questions clamouring for an answer.

\* \* \* \* \* \* \*

Clay did not know how long a time elapsed before he became aware of living beings. At first he was apparently an object of curiosity. Men and women, both sexes remarkably handsome and clearly highly intelligent, came and studied him and talked to each other in a language he could not understand.

These people were dressed in the lightest of clothes, which emphasised the masculine ruggedness of the men and the symphonic curves of the women. So Clay just lay rigid and stared dummy-like at whatever came in line with his vision—until finally he was picked up, placed upon some kind of conveyance, and borne into the heart of the tall, spired city.

Since Clay could only look upward and slightly forwards, his view was limited to the building tops, the sky, and finally the high, glazed ceiling of an immense room. Here were scientists—or at least they appeared to be—for Clay caught a glimpse of instruments, and it occurred to him that he must be in some sort of hospital or operating theatre.

There was a low murmur of musical voices, and with all that was in him Clay tried to speak—but his tongue would not move a fraction of an inch. Finally one of the men came forward and looked him straight in the eyes. He had blue eyes, Clay noticed—intensely blue indeed and extremely steady. And the longer they gazed, the more Clay realized that these eyes were the only things in the whole crazy setup that made any sense. They were lulling—compelling....

Suddenly the man with the eyes seemed to speak. It

took Clay only a fraction of a second to realize that his mind had made contact with the Other.

"My friend, I have no idea who you are or from where you have come, but just try and understand my communication. This is hypnosis, the only method by which I can penetrate the barrier. Do you understand hypnosis?"

"A little." Clay's response was only mental, but evidently it was readily grasped.

"That is excellent. I am a surgeon and mental specialist.... Who are you? What is the matter with you? Your case resembles extreme catalepsy or advanced suspended animation, yet it seems to be something more profound than even those."

Thus given the opportunity, Clay concentrated as hard as he could on the entire sequence of his experiences. Without interruption, Clay's universe limited to the steady stare of the blue eyes, the hypnotist listened. When Clay had come nearly to the end of 'thinking' his narrative his emotions got the better of him.

"I believe I am dead—that this world is beyond death, or something like it. I am motionless. I do not seem to breathe. My heart does not seem to beat. I just don't understand!"

The scientist gave a slow, grave smile. "Your problem, my friend. is not so complex to me, a man of science—and a science far ahead of yours, apparently—as it is to you.... What you have to realize is that your body is still in the same condition that the attainment of Absolute Zero imposed upon it. But your mind—as distinct from *brain*—being non-material, it has not conformed to the laws of Absolute Zero and therefore is alert. What you see around you is actually your own world, but a different aspect of it."

"My own world! I still do not understand!"

"Then I will put it this way: Your scientific belief is that complete cessation of molecular activity produces the nearest approach to matter-death. Right?"

"I have always believed that to be the case," Clay admitted. "In fact, everybody does."

"That belief is incorrect. You base your belief on what you believe is Absolute Zero. For obvious reasons you can only determine the position of Zero by considering your own unit of time-measurement, the measurement to which you are accustomed. Let me cite the simple instance, familiar to you, of certain insects in your own plane to whom a lifetime is but one or two of your days....

"Their time-unit is totally different from yours: their conception of Zero would be very different from yours if they were capable of thinking of it. In this case, therefore, you have reached the Absolute Zero of your measurement, only to find that there is life and movement just the same, but on a different time-ratio.... Compared to you, we move with inconceivable slowness. Your plane, relative to ours, moves with prodigious swiftness. From what you have told me, you saw—as one facet of your transition—coastal erosion, the work of ages, occurring in a matter of seconds. That is the proof of my statement. It is possible that your body is alive, my friend, but that it is functioning so slowly in this plane that a mere blink of the eyelid would take several of our years to accomplish! So you feel, and appear, motionless, because your normally fast reactions are slowed down immeasurably by the vibratory conditions existing here."

For a long interval Clay meditated over the things he had been told, then he continued.

"We acknowledge in my plane that matter vibrates at different speeds. And we acknowledge, too, that some insects pass through a lifetime in one of our days. But none of us ever conceived the possibility of a living plane at our measure of Absolute Zero."

"Yet here it is." the scientist said. "For further proof I would mention a golden band in our sky...."

"I saw that," Clay interrupted. "What is it? A disintegrated moon or something?"

"Certainly not. Your plane has no disintegrated moon, has it? Why should ours? This is still Earth, remember. No, the golden arc you have seen is the sun. You see it, I gather, as a globe moving sedately across the heavens. To us it moves with such terrific speed that it is always a band of light, persistence of vision giving it an arcing effect from horizon to horizon. The arc is perpetual, varying only in height according to the seasons. Otherwise we have eternal day."

Very gradually Clay was commencing to realize how right this scientist was, how incontestable his evidence. And it also gave Clay a sidelight upon the almost incredible diversity of Nature, in that she provides life even at what we consider to be the limit of material movement.

"I suppose," Clay resumed presently, still using only his mind for communication, "that I am actually still in the same space as before, except for having been removed to this laboratory, only my plane cannot be seen because of its terrific speed, any more than one can see the individual spokes of a fast-turning wheel? Just as we cannot see your plane because of its extreme slowness?"

"Exactly so. You cannot see both heat and light, can you?—yet they both travel at the same speed. The difference is in the wavelength. Between this plane and yours the difference is in vibration. Our slowness and your speed makes both our planes able to exist one within the other without interference. Only when one crosses the borderline, which is evidently Absolute Zero on your scale, is it possible to move from one plane to the other."

"Every blink of the eyelids takes me years; every breath takes centuries," Clay 'said', reverting to the personal enigma. "What am I to do, then? I want to be one of you, to live and move and see this new-found world. Don't you realize the immensity of the thing I have done? Surely there ought to be some reward for that?"

Clay saw hesitation come into the mesmeric eyes. "Naturally we appreciate what you have done, and the enormous risk you took, but I doubt if there is anything we can do for you. Your type of matter is totally different in molecular construction from ours. Ours at this vibratory plane is normal; yours is vastly retarded."

"But I can't stay like this! You are a scientist and you say your knowledge is far ahead of mine. There ought to be some way of overcoming the difficulty."

"Yes...there ought." The scientist brooded for a time; then, "I shall give the problem every consideration. I will consult with my colleagues. I think it only fair to tell you, though, that this world of ours is dying. Before very long we shall seek another planet, or else go underground. The sun is expiring. Do not forget that to us a split second is a century to you. In the aggregate that means that, from our point of view, the sun is losing mass and dying at a tremendous pace."

"Why do you tell me this?" Clay asked.

"I tell you because if we can revive you, there would not be much point in it. You would find little here for which to stay. Merely a matter of survival."

"Even that would be preferable to this ghastly fixation."

Then Clay became silent because he was becoming conscious of a disquieting fact. Time cannot be reversed: that is fundamental law. Since he had come—albeit unintentionally—to this plane, his own plane must now be hundreds of centuries behind him! If he could ever get back there with this particular material body, he would find all that he had known and cherished lost in the mists of dim antiquity.... Something else also occurred to him. He had probably vanished completely from the A-Z Chamber. Or had he? Which plane was he vibrating to? This one or his own?

"This one," the scientist answered, as Clay questioned him; "The fact that you are visible to us proves it. In your own plane you will be invisible and be presumed to have disappeared. Not that it matters now, I'm afraid, for countless centuries have gone since you vanished from the A-Z Chamber. You vanished from it the moment you came in 'sympathy' with this plane. But you are not of this plane, therefore your molecular makeup cannot change, but continues to perform the actions with the speed normal to it—that is years to blink an eyelid, and so on. You are like a vehicle trying to move with the brakes on."

"Something," Clay insisted, "has got to be done—and I feel reasonably convinced that you can do it. It would obviously do me no good to return to my own plane, so use every scrap of knowledge you have got to make me a worthwhile member of this one."

The scientist nodded slowly. "Believe me, my friend, we will do all we can."

* * * * * * *

To Clay it seemed fantastic never to need sleep or food—for so incredibly low was his energy expenditure he did not need anything to replenish it. It was even more fantastic to never be aware of breathing air, to live in a ratio utterly alien to the surroundings. Nor did the fact that he was removed to a private room and given several robots to await on any need he might have, make the position any easier. All he really wanted was movement and life. It was infuriating to have made such a fortuitous journey beyond the Zero limit to find himself physically incapable of taking advantage of it. He was convinced that this mighty civilization held a great deal of interest: he was also convinced that he could offer a considerable amount of information concerning his own plane.

Yet here he was—motionless, dead yet alive, robots within range of his thoughts and responding to them if so needed. Nothing was wanted—except liberty.

At intervals the master-scientist called and exchanged grave communications in the usual semi-hypnotic way. So far, it seemed, he and his colleagues had not made much progress towards finding a way of liberating Clay—but they were still hopeful.

"There could not be a more bitter irony," Clay declared. "To have done something no human being ever did before and be unable to move! Do you suppose that is some kind of punishment for my having violated a law of Nature?"

There was faint amusement in the scientist's thoughts. "That could hardly be, my friend, because you made the journey by accident. You did not plan this thing: it was thrust upon you. I can appreciate your chagrin, but do not give up hope. We are working now on a possible solution to the riddle."

"When will you know the answer?"

"I cannot say exactly. Very soon. Meanwhile I observe that monotony is wearying you. I will do what

I can to alleviate that for you."

The master-scientist was as good as his word. He sent more robots to Clay, which, by virtue of their particular capacities, showed him three-dimensional pictures in colour motion. From them Clay gained a cross-sectional viewpoint of a thriving, industrious, peace-loving civilization. existing beyond the normal conception of Absolute Zero—a world wherein science was used purely for mutual benefit, but where everything was so utterly foreign that Clay's whole being cried out for a return to his own plane, no matter how changed it might have become in the interval.

It was, of course, impossible for him to even begin to assess the basic laws of these people, or their science. Their measurements all began where 'normal' ones end. Their method of reckoning Time was quite incomprehensible to Clay. Their existence was threatened by the sun's hurtling rush into extinction—whereas Clay was accustomed to the sun's decline being measured only in the ponderous march of centuries, cycles, and aeons.

So here, then, was the amazing paradox of a civilization superb in knowledge, yet which could not be understood. Clay was quite satisfied that the robot machines showed him everything about the 'Beyond Zero' race—their social order, their science, the ever-present shadow of extinction—and yet at the end of it he still did not understand a thing about them, nor could he unless he became one of them. He realized that one cannot shift from one plane to another and form comparison. It was to him as though every law of mathematics had been disavowed.

That everything is relative Clay had never appreciated more clearly. His body, refusing to function to this plane's vibration, was relative to only one—the one from which he had come and into which he had been born....

Then came a time when the master-scientist returned, seating himself so that he was directly in Clay's line of vision. As usual, his hypnotic power transmitted a message.

"My colleagues and I have investigated your unique problem very closely, my friend, and we are willing to make an experiment to bring you in tune with our rate of vibration. I say we are willing. Whether that willingness will be shared by you only you can say."

"Anything is better than this," Clay responded. "I want to live, and move, and be one of you—form the bridge between one plane and another. If *I* can be restored—or altered to conform with the conditions—others may come after me if I can communicate with them."

"True," the scientist admitted; "but I should not place too much store on that possibility. You have to remember the speeding centuries in your own plane.... However, that is not an immediate concern. If you are prepared for our experiment?"

"Entirely."

The scientist nodded and got to his feet. He turned to the nearby attendant robots—which so far had not been used—and gave them mental instructions. In response they glided forward, raised Clay's rigid, motionless body in their delicate, pincer-like hands, and thereafter transported him with extreme care from the private room and down the long corridor outside, the master-scientist in the lead.

The journey ended in a surgical laboratory, and Clay found himself laid upon a broad table. As usual, he lay motionless, and after a moment the master-scientist's face appeared to his vision. In a matter of seconds hypnotic communication was once more established.

"I must warn you, my friend, that this is a gamble with your life. If you die, the blame will attach entirely to us. I can only say, in advance, that we have made every possible computation and are reasonably sure of success."

"Go right ahead," Clay responded. "If I die, I'll at least find liberation from this bodily prison. Consider how *I* feel. If it takes me centuries to even blink an eyelid, how long is my natural span of life going to extend? Almost to eternity! I prefer death if I am to have it."

The scientist smiled gravely. "We will do our best," he promised, and then his face vanished from Clay's viewpoint.

There was an interval and a variety of strange sounds, some of which Clay interpreted as electrical; then powerful shadowless globes came into being, blasting everything into a quivering halo of brilliance.

No anaesthetics were used and Clay might as well

have been dead for all the sensation he felt as instruments went to work upon him. As far as he could judge, most of them were electrical. This was not surgery in the accepted sense, but an experiment to change the range of his electron metabolism, thereby fitting him into the conditions in which he found himself.

It seemed an interminable time passed, during which he felt no particular change; then the probing and instrument work ceased and the face of the master-scientist reappeared. It was drawn and troubled.

"I am afraid," he said quietly, "that we have to admit failure. There is nothing wrong with our instruments, nor anything wrong with our procedure. The factor that defeats us is Time. Time is an abstract thing, yet fundamental in all our calculations. We cannot reason out the necessary variations for dealing with a body like yours, built to operate in a time-ratio totally different from ours."

Clay did not concentrate upon an answer. Indeed, he could not: he was too utterly depressed by the news.

"All we can do," the scientist added, "is fit you out with the necessary compensators and thereby enable you to seem to live at our ratio."

"How do you mean?" Clay asked, after an interval.

"I mean that one instrument can be fitted which will pick up your thoughts and translate them into vocal sounds—whereby you will appear to speak. Another instrument on universal mountings can be fitted to your skull and be attached electronically to your brain by which you will be able to see in any direction you choose without the necessity of turning your head.... In short, we can make of you a mechanical man, understanding everything of this plane by means of compensating equipment whilst you yourself will never move. That I fear, is the utmost we can do for you. It might make your position a little more tolerable."

Since, apparently, it was the only conceivable way out of the difficulty, Clay did not raise any objections. He allowed the scientists to go to work on him again and, as before, he had no sensation whatever as they fitted the various electronic devices and drove vibration-carrying wires deep into his skull—until at last the modifications were complete.

"Now," came the master scientist's concentrations, "you have only to *think*, my friend, and these devices will take care of everything. If you *think* you would like to see what is transpiring around you, observe what happens."

Though he barely understood, Clay was quite willing to obey. Accordingly, he thought of how much he would like to see this laboratory, of which he had so far seen only the ceiling—and almost instantly there came before his vision a level view of the instruments, the scientists, the wall beyond them. The whole setup on a normal horizontal plane.

"That's better!" Clay concentrated, and to his surprise he heard his voice actually say the words.

"Thoughts transformed into vibratory air waves." the master-scientist explained. "Thereby producing what sounds to be a voice. Naturally, your thoughts take shape in your own language—in which I am also speaking. In case you wonder how I have picked it up so quickly, please remember that I have searched your mentality pretty considerably since you came here, and your language is one of the least difficult factors to assimilate."

"Can you give me a simulation of walking?" Clay asked. "I would welcome anything except this constant paralysis."

"*Think* what you would like to do," came the grave response.

Clay did as he was bidden, and to his surprise he found it possible to rise into a sitting position, descend from the table, and then start walking clumsily. He looked down at himself—or imagined he did—and then realized it was the complex device that acted as his eyes which was operating. He beheld queer stilt-like attachments on his legs by which means he was able to walk about, albeit stumblingly.

"I realize you are but a travesty of a man," the scientist said, "but it may make life easier for you. Nothing can go wrong and everything you do is at the dictate of your mind."

Clay walked around for a while, accustoming himself, the scientists watching him—then he came back to questioning.

"If everything I do is so at the dictate of my mind, why should I be limited to this particular plane?"

"A strange question," the master-scientist observed, frowning.

"I mean this body you have patched up—which in all normal circumstances might be regarded as dead—is now made to walk, talk, and see purely by the dictate of my mind. Can I not make it return to my own plane by mind force alone?"

The scientists looked at one another, then at the instrument-supported man they had 'resurrected.'

"You admit, surely, that there is no barrier to mind?" Clay demanded. "It can hurdle one plane as easily as another, so why cannot it transfer me back home?"

"That, my friend, would be the absolute mastery of mind over matter, and we do not believe you have that much power or control. Even we haven't, and we are ahead of you."

"I can try," Clay said, and thereupon threw himself into an immense effort of concentration, the effect of which was at once both unnerving and extraordinary.

Through the auditory system that had been fitted to his brain he seemed to hear voices—one vast noisy cacophony which reminded him of a dozen radio sets all talking at once. At the same instant his eyes beheld not only the laboratory in which he was standing but also some kind of fabulous city beyond it—superimposed. It was gigantic in architecture, its mighty streets bridged by metal viaducts across which at varying levels moved vehicles and. people. It was a complex, shattering pattern, which made Clay wince helplessly.

"If you find your sensations unendurable," came the voice of the master-scientist, "press the button on your breastplate and return everything to neutral." Clay could not move his hand, but he willed himself to move the neutralising button, and immediately a gentle, flexible tentacle attached to the instrument about his waist moved the switch concerned. The visions and the screaming din of a myriad voices and unwanted sounds faded out. There was a great, restful calm that spread over Clay's consciousness like a healing balm.

"That's better." he found himself saying, and the master-scientist came across to him.

"Do you realize what happened, my friend?"

"No. It was like hell itself whilst it lasted."

"What you saw was your own plane, dove-tailed into this one. Your natural body was immediately in sympathy with it, whilst the instruments attached to you gave you cognizance of this plane. The result was that your personality—or at least your mind—was divided over the two states. The result was most unpleasant. You are probably thinking of your own plane and Time as being infinitely far away, like something on another world, but that is not so. It is *here*, next door to us, hidden only by its vibratory speed. For a moment you glimpsed and heard it whilst still actually here...."

"Then why can I not make that short step which would take me from here to there? What is in the way?"

"The mathematical problem of vibration," the scientist replied. "Imagine it this way. Between you and a valuable jewel there is an electric fan moving at top revolution. Can you see that fan? No. You will feel the wind from it, yes—but for the purpose of our analogy let us assume you cannot. Now, the fan blades are revolving so swiftly there appears to be only a fine mist between you and that jewel. And if you attempted to seize that jewel through the mist, what then? Your material hand would be slashed to ribbons.... So it is here. There is a veil between—the veil of vibration."

"But I came *here*," Clay insisted. "Why can't the process be reversed to send me back?"

"Because we do not understand the mathematics which reduced you to the below zero condition. We only understand our *own* mathematics, and they are not applicable to your type of life."

Clay reflected. "There must be a way back. I'm a scientific engineer, so maybe I'll work something out...."

\* \* \* \* \* \* \*

So Clay returned to the room that had been provided for him. It was a relief to be able to pilot his body about by means of mental impulses, even though the exact processes involved were completely beyond him. Most intriguing of all to him, however, was the recollection of that superimposed view he had had of his own plane and this other one beyond zero. It had shown him one thing: despite the tremendous lapse of Time that had ensued in his own plane, life still existed there—and indeed it was probably at the absolute zenith of its development. If he could only return now, he would be in a world where absolute perfection probably reigned, where the scientific dreams of his own day had become facts. Space travel would be an everyday thing, perhaps even perpetual motion, destruction of crime and disease—all those things had perhaps come to pass.

He had *got* to return. There was no longer any doubt about it. It was a yearning that passed all control. He had seen all there was to see in this strange beyond-zero land, and had gathered enough to realize it was a civilization that he would never be completely able to understand.... So back he must go.

At first with extreme caution, he again tried the experiment of viewing his own plane, and once again there burst upon him the ear-shattering clamour of a million sounds. This time he switched out the auditory machines responsible for hearing, and dead silence blanked him. Thus he was better able to concentrate on the visual aspect.

Already it had changed from the previous scene. The giant city he had formerly viewed had given place to one of much smaller dimensions, though it was plainly still one of superb architecture. Lying on his bed he surveyed it, apparently hanging beyond the wall of his room; then gradually his attention shifted to a mighty statue of glittering metal surmounting the tallest building in the city. The more he studied it, the more surprised he became.

Either it was a colossal coincidence or else that statue was identical in face to Nick Farrish!

But how could that be? Nick Farrish must have been dead for hundreds of years, so it could only be a remarkable resemblance and nothing else. And yet....

The mystery obsessed Clay completely, and because he had no logical answer for it he finally sent one of the attendant robots to summon the master-scientist. He came immediately, as courteous and willing to help as ever. Briefly Clay explained the problem, his view of his own plane now neutralised by the special cut-out switch.

"Obviously," he finished, "it isn't possible. Probably my imagination playing tricks."

"Not necessarily," the scientist answered, thinking. "The matter puzzles you only because your grasp of science is not so profound as ours—or mine. For instance, what do you know of death and that which follows it?"

"There are many theories in my plane about that. Some say we go on living in another form; some say it is utter oblivion. For myself I've no fixed idea."

"Well, we have, my friend, and I pass it on to you as an absolute fact because we have scientifically proved it. Here is your answer— A living body is the material outline of a mental concept. In other words, you and everybody else has a mental conception of what the body—your own particular body—is like. When death comes, the mentality does not die: it cannot because it is not material, and only material things die. It is a law of Nature that a material body becomes old and wears out. When that happens the mind, compelled to express itself through some physical vestment or other, immediately forms a new body. And naturally that new body must look identical to the one before it because the mental conception of it has not changed. You understand so far?"

"I think so," Clay acknowledged. "So we are born again with a body that will grow to be identical to the previous one."

"Usually after three days. It takes that long—by your reckoning of time—for the change to be completed. Nor is it always necessary for the new body to appear in the same locality as that in which the old one died. Very rarely, in fact, because in the interval time and space have moved.... So, then. to resolve your problem. This statue probably is of your friend, several lifetimes removed from the time when you knew him. Even in your day he was obviously a brilliant scientist, and since mental accomplishments do not die when the body dies, it stands to reason that by now he must be a superb genius of his art. Why not even the leading scientist of the world, which would account for him being acclaimed by a statue?"

"Then," Clay said slowly, "if I could somehow reach that period I can see, I could meet him again? Or at least his latest concept of himself, if I can call it such?"

"No doubt of it."

Clay was silent for a moment, then, "Don't think me rude, sir, but I wish to be left alone, to concentrate. If, as you say, the mind can force the body to do anything, I am going to try and discover for myself if Nick really is to be found...."

The scientist smiled gravely, got to his feet, and left the room. Clay lay silent for a while, then switching out the auditory control once more he resumed his view of the city...and several more years had already slipped by. He could tell that by the smears of age which had appeared on the buildings, and the statue too, formerly so glittering, now revealed distinct signs of tarnish.

Presently Clay began to test the power of his mentality. He ordered his body forward, and insofar as the instruments controlling him could manage it he was impelled apparently much nearer to the city—but he could not enter it. Between him and it there still loomed that unbreakable barrier of vibration between planes. Nonetheless, projected like an astral presence, he was close enough to the men and women of this future time in his own plane to be able to study them and watch their comings and goings.

But this was not what he wanted. He wanted to see if the original of the statue really was a futuristic Nick Farrish—and this was a task that kept him occupied almost continuously since he never needed either sleep or food....

Eventually his wandering on the edge of his own future-time plane brought its reward. He came to the verge of a great public demonstration, viewing it as though through a sheet of glass, unable to take part in it, yet watching every detail.... And, addressing the multitude in an amphitheatre as colossal as anything ever produced by ancient Rome, was a uniformed being of obviously high standing, and he was Nick Farrish.

Clay watched him intently, then he took the risk of switching on the auditory mechanism. Normally he received the battering din of the city and a myriad voices, but this time—as he had hoped—the city was muted and the traffic stilled so that the voice of this one being, obviously the leader, could be heard without interruption over a worldwide radio network.

"...and the conquest is therefore complete." Clay switched in on mid-sentence and wondered what had gone before. "It is the mightiest accomplishment of all, my people. We conquered the inner planets long ago—not without sacrifice and fatalities, it is true— and now the outer worlds are ours. Earth is dominant and we are the masters of the entire solar system. Let that never be forgotten, I have lived for many, many centuries to see this day dawn, and I will live many centuries more to see the consummation of the project we have commenced...."

There came a murmur of assent from assembled thousands and Clay continued to listen.

"To have lived as I have, through two thousand years, is an accomplishment worthy of attempting. You all know me as the Eternal One because I found the way to prevent death. But wisely I kept the secret to myself so I could be your leader. That I have tried to be to the best of my ability.... Nor have I ever allowed my heart to rule my head. Where I have seen a possible division of power, the chance of myself and some other scientist knowing as much as each other, I have stamped out the opposition. Wisely, I believe. Two cannot rule: only one. Far back in the beginning of my ageless life, before I discovered the mutational secret of immortality, there was one who could have rivalled me in scientific knowledge, but by a lucky accident I was able to dispose of him. At that time we were experimenting with below-zero temperatures, and he explored the special zero-chamber without my permission or knowledge. He was not aware that I had kept an eye on him, that I feared he might be a danger to my own scientific advancement—so when the chance came, I closed him within the freezing chamber and threw the switch. He was never seen again....

"And why do I tell you this? To show you that I am a ruthless man; to show you that I will stamp out without mercy the slightest breath of opposition. And also to show you that none can equal your leader in power and knowledge. And I—"

Clay switched off the auditory power, and then pressed the neutralising button. Returned to his 'normal' state of torpor he lay thinking, wondering, piecing together the astounding speech be had heard. It had to be believed, because Nick Farrish himself had spoken the words. It meant then that Nick *had* known that he, Clay, had been inside the A.Z Chamber and he had deliberately murdered him. Or thought he had. Because he had had no intention of sharing his scientific skill with any man!

And how skilled he must have become, too, to solve the riddle of eternal life and by that very reason become master of the Earth. This was not a reincarnated Nick Farrish. It was the same man—hard, cold, scientific, absolute master of himself and the world. Yet not clever enough to realize that his one-time best friend had *not* died but still lived, automatically moved on in Time by vibratory process and keeping pace. Keeping pace! If only there were a way to break through— To avenge! Clay strove to express his emotional fury by clenching his fists, but no vestige of movement escaped him voluntarily and, for the moment, the obedient mechanisms were in neutral.

The scene was changed—immensely, immeasurably changed. And Clay now was governed only by one obsession. To come face to face with Nick before the speeding centuries and the death of the world made contact forever impossible.... Once again Clay sent for the master-scientist and explained the situation.

"Somehow," Clay insisted, "you have got to project me through the barrier back to my own plane. Reverse the process which brought me here."

"It is impossible without the basic mathematics."

"I'll give some of them to you—as many as I was personally involved with. Listen carefully...."

Calling on every vestige of his memory, made doubly clear by the urgency governing him. Clay gave the details insofar as he could remember them, after which the scientist departed to feed the figures into the mathematical transmutation machines, which would convert the figures into the below-zero values. Evidently the feat was successful, for eventually the master-scientist came back, smiling triumphantly.

"We have enough to go upon, my friend. We shall build another A-Z globe, using vibratory forces equally balanced to speed the molecular rate into what—to us—will be the limit of activity. When the highest attainable vibration is reached, your body will cross the barrier.... But, my friend, have you thought of the Time which is speeding by in your own plane?"

"Certainly I have. Hence the urgency."

"Very well. The globe will be constructed immediately."

With the instruments and equipment at his command, it did not take the master-scientist above two normal days to have the globe made. Then Clay was brought to it, his various aid-instruments were removed, and he was laid inside a chamber identical to the one in which he had made his original journey. Once the trap shut, he was again in that awful, crushing darkness reminiscent of the time when he had searched for his cigarette case.

Evidently, the electro-magnetic vibratory apparatus was at work, for after a while a real conviction of sensation began to steal over him as locked molecules responded. It was like being restored from a deadening attack of cramp. He began to tingle, to feel warm—even comfortable. But the sensation was short-lived and fear reared its ugly head again. He was becoming cold. Surely the process had not reversed itself halfway?

It was a coldness which increased instead of abating, but at the same time the darkness was relieved by glowing points of light which came one by one out of the abyss and winked at him in frosty calm. He was watching them appear, wondering why they didn't change position, when it dawned upon him that he had the power of movement again. He scrambled up, realizing that the enclosing walls of the globe had gone, and with it that other plane, the master-scientists, everything!

Clay was in some great wild, rocky space. A wind, thin and cruel, bit deep into his lungs and set him coughing, flapping his tattered, old-world clothing. He turned dumbly, staring about him. A mile away, perhaps, were countless little lights, occasionally obscured as something passed before them. This was the only sign of life. Otherwise the landscape was undisturbed and black under the hard, merciless stars. The great diadem of heaven was like an inverted bowl overhead.

The air was deadly thin. It stung. It choked. Clay knew he was dying—but the lights in the distance fascinated him and he moved towards them, his feet dragging. Once or twice he saw a group of the lights flash skywards in a creaming flare of exhaust. Spaceships were taking off, probably from a world that was on the very edge of extinction, one face turned forever to the sun and the other to the night.

Clay went on, thinking of the measureless centuries that had passed, of the engulfment of Man's handiwork in the crushing maw of Time. There were only these departing spaceships, the steely stars, the searing wind. Clay's mind drifted back to a world as it had been—sunshine, soft breezes, progress, the joy of companionship. Friends—! Friends? What of Nick Farrish?

He went on again. Yes, the objects were spaceships. He could see each one individually now—hundreds of them in a great circle under the stars. And, in the centre of the circle they created there were vast mountains of equipment.

Clay dragged further forwards, passed under the nose of the nearest monster of the void, and came into the circle. He reeled helplessly from lack of air and piercing cold.... The next thing he knew he was warm and comfortable, and about him were the curved walls of a space machine's interior. The serious faces of men and women, all of them in uniforms similar to the one Nick Farrish had been wearing, looked down upon him.

"Whence come you?" one of the men asked. "Know you not this is Earth? Know you not this is the last day on which we shall stay? We go to claim the conquest of the other worlds."

Clay smiled bitterly. His heart was labouring.

"I—I must speak to the Eternal," he muttered.

The men and women glanced at each other, then one of the men darted off, presently returning with the unmistakable Nick Farrish, wrapped to the ears in furs. He stared in blank, even horrified amazement—and Clay stared back. The lines and creases of immeasurable age were bitten as if by acid into Nick's face.

"I—I have been a long time returning from Absolute Zero, Nick," Clay muttered, fighting for breath, "but I finally managed it.... Not as successful as you thought, were you?"

Nick did not reply. A remarkable expression crossed his face, followed by a look of intense pain. He said something inaudible, then clutching at his breast with an enormous heated glove he toppled forward and hit the floor.

Nobody spoke—but one of the women moved.

"It is unbelievable," Clay heard her whispering. "The Eternal One is dead! How could that happen? He had no shock of any kind, and as he once told us, only shock could ever destroy him by breaking the delicate muscle fibres controlling his heart. He had no shock, and yet he is dead."

"And we are free," the man muttered. his eyes gleaming. "Do you not realize what it means, Ania? The Eternal is dead! The despotism is no more! The tyranny, the heartbreaks, the hand of the oppressor— And yet to die without shock after thousands of years of life. It is not scientifically feasible."

"Wait," the woman murmured. "Perhaps our visitor—"

She crossed to Clay and looked at him intently. He opened drowsy eyes and smiled.

"Friend, who are you?" The touch of her feminine hands felt good to Clay. "Whence came you? Why did the Eternal look at you and die? You have brought us freedom from a seemingly endless despotism. When we reach the other worlds we can live in security and happiness. What is the answer, visitor? You have liberated the entire race of Earth and we must know why! What did the Eternal see in you?"

"Vengeance, perhaps," Clay whispered. "A spirit down the ageless centuries, maybe. The pointing finger...." He knew he was rambling. The scene around him was fading.

"You gave us liberty," the woman insisted; then the tall man beside her caught her arm and gently raised her.

"Waste no more time, Ania," he murmured gently. "There is no gain in talking to a corpse."

# ACROSS THE AGES

As I recall, the business started when Len Brownson, Greg Smith, and I were rooming together in New York. All three of us were in the same line of business—radio-television and electronics; all of us were pretty much of an age and got along famously together.

Anyway, Greg and I did. We liked baseball and girls—nothing serious though—and the movies and television.... So did Len Brownson for about a year of our companionship, then the oddest change suddenly came over him.

At the best of times, he was a moody, introspective sort of chap, dark-eyed, with a mop of black tumbling hair that was never brought to order. Quite different from Greg and me: we are blue-eyed, short-necked specimens of the Saxon variety.

I wonder if you have ever come home from a rattling good evening to find a pale-faced, dark young man sitting in the dark before the window, gazing out onto the heavens over the rooftops? Maybe not, but that's the way we found Len on the evening of last October 24th. I remember the date well.

Just for a moment, my flesh crawled. The faint light

from reflected signs caught the parchment white of Len's skin. His face looked like that of a ghost. His eyes were black pools against it; his hair had fallen over his forehead. From the way his hands clutched the sides of his chair, I thought for a moment he'd contracted catalepsy or something.

Then, with his usual tactlessness, Greg switched on the lights.

"Say, what the heck's going on in here?" he demanded. "Snap out of it, Len! What's the idea of sitting in the dark?"

Len turned ever so slightly to look at us. "Have you never liked to sit in the dark?" he asked. He had a quiet, mellow sort of voice.

"Only when there's a dame with me," Greg grinned, and winked as he glanced across at me. Finally, as silence persisted, he straddled a chair and faced Len directly.

"What's wrong?" he demanded bluntly. "You cried off coming along with us tonight—said you'd work to do. Don't tell me this was it!"

It struck me, standing a bit to one side, that Len did not even hear the question. He was still staring out of the window, way out to where the stars were shining

"Tonight," he said at last, slowly, "I begin to understand. Just imagine it! The slow procession of the centuries—ages, generations. Countless lives, countless people, and yet—reincarnation! One day it must come again. That same being must return, to love and live again. Must finish that which was formerly undone...."

"Huh?" Greg's face was almost comical in its amazement. "What—what the hell are you raving about, Len?"

He got up, disgruntled, and ambled into the kitchen. I half turned to follow him, then hesitated. I stopped in front of Len and regarded him seriously. After a while, his deep, dark eyes glanced up at me. I admit they gave me a bit of a shock. There was a light in them such as I have never seen before or since—a deep, unearthly light, as though he were looking into things beyond the earthly veil.

"You think I'm crazy, eh?" he asked, smiling faintly.

I shrugged. "I know you're OK, Len—a regular fellow.... But I'm a bit puzzled, naturally."

"Sit down a moment." He motioned to Greg's abandoned chair.

"You have a bit more imagination than Greg," he said, as I sat gazing at him. "He's a grand chap, but—well, you know! You may understand.... She is waiting for me. She has been waiting, for tens of thousands of years. I know now that worlds have lived and died while she has waited, locked, at her own wish, deep within her tomb...."

I think I swallowed something. Certainly I could not speak.

"She knew that one day I would come back," he went on, his voice a droning monotone. "By the law of chance I must come back! To think that there could be such a love as hers—that she could wait through endless centuries. Sleeping, not dead—sleeping in the ruins of a world and city that once were great. I know she lives and that her mind is bridging the gulf from her world to Earth. I know because at last I feel what she is trying to tell me!

"Yes, that is why I am sitting here, concentrating, thinking, brooding. Mentally I can see her, locked in her mausoleum. There is only one way in, and I am the only man who knows that way. But first I must reach her world...."

He stopped talking. He was breathing hard from his emotions; a light perspiration had gathered on his face. Greg had come in with an apron tucked by the corners into his waistcoat pockets, two plates in his hands. As he heard the last bit he screwed up his pug nose.

"Say, is this a nut house or an apartment for three technicians?" he demanded.

"Mars...," Len breathed. "That is her world."

Dead silence descended on all of us at that. Then, suddenly, Len sprang to his feet, looked at Greg and me with blazing eyes. "Don't you understand?" he demanded, with a desperation that was somehow uncomfortable to witness. "I have to go to Mars—to her!"

"Oh, yeah—sure," Greg nodded consolingly, looking at me. "We'll fix it for you all right—same way as they fix Napoleon and Abe Lincoln," he added sourly. "Quit fooling, Len! Supper's nearly ready and—"

"You—you dunderhead!" Len shouted hoarsely, suddenly gripping the astonished Greg by the wrists.

"You think this is a joke? I mean it—every word of it! You are my friends, the only two in the world who understand me.... This is something tremendous, so tremendous I only half understand it myself. To me has been given a secret—space travel!"

"What!" I yelled, jumping up.

"I mean it!" he cried earnestly; and it was comforting to see something of that weird intensity drop from him. "I realized it this evening for the first time. For weeks I've been trying to get it, and now tonight— Came all in a rush! Maybe the conditions were better for telepathy—"

"Telepathy? Space travel?" Greg's mouth was an O of amazement. "B-but how the heck can we build a spaceship, here?"

"Who said anything about a spaceship?" Len snapped.

"You said it, you dope—"

"I said nothing about a ship. I shall reach Mars because no earthly power can hold me back. It is the inevitable law of chance that must operate. Earth is not my real home. I realize it now. I am as inevitably a part of Mars as you two are of Earth.... Oh, it's all so complex! If only you'd try to understand."

"I'll say it's complex!" Greg snorted, dumping the plates down. "I think you're plain screwy— 'Scuse me, the stew's boiling over."

He dashed back into the kitchen and left me looking at Len in curiosity. Quietly, he laid a hand on my arm.

"Really, it's the truth," he said seriously. "To explain

it now with the thing only half-done is next to impossible, but I believe there may be a way. Tonight—probably in about six hours—I shall go to Mars. I know that with absolute certainty. Don't be alarmed, Dick—it just has to be. When the adventure is over, I'll see to it that you know the whole truth. Somehow I'll get word to you—from Mars."

"You ask me to believe a lot," I muttered. "I guess I'm your friend, and—well, don't blame me for disbelieving you. It's so crazy!" I insisted. "For instance, what is this law of chance you keep talking about? What the hell is it?"

He shrugged. "As near as I can tell you now, it means that if a certain set of conditions, bodily conditions, exactly fit another set of conditions, there must be a dissolution from the state that is wrong to the one that is right. Can you figure that out?"

I scratched my head over it. "Damned if I can!" I said. "Maybe we'll get it clearer when you get to Mars," I grinned.

He did not smile back at me. That light of strange wisdom had come back into his dark eyes.

It was like having supper with a ghost that evening. Len hardly said a word as he ate, kept his eyes fixed on the window. Once he burst into a frenzy when Greg moved over to draw the shade down.... Greg returned to the table with concern written all over his face. Time and again he glanced at me—but what could I do? I felt just as uncomfortable and uneasy as he did.

We got to bed at last, I had promised myself that I

would keep awake and watch for anything that might happen. The three of us had separate beds, Greg between Len and me. I know Len was awake a long time, staring at the sky signs flashing out their incessant glares through the night.

Then I guess I dozed. From remote distances, it seemed, I heard one or two strange noises. I was conscious too of a cold such as I have never known before or since. It felt like solid ice ramming down my back.... With a slamming heart I awoke violently.

I saw something I shall never forget—and Greg saw it too.

The pair of us sat shuddering with cold, gazing at the incredible sight of a transparent Len floating slowly from his bed toward the window! He was apparently asleep, motionless with his arms at his sides, bare feet out-thrust from the legs of his pyjamas.

In blank horror we waited for the smashing of the window glass—but none came! He went through the solid glass like a wraith. Out, out, over the now darkened roofs toward the pale dawn.... We could see him for a while becoming even more transparent. Then he was gone!

As he went, the fearful cold relaxed. Shaking with fright and reaction, Greg and I fell back on our beds, too stunned to speak or move.

Naturally, Greg and I discussed the horrible night for weeks afterward. And we had the practical side to deal with too. At first we got into a pretty stiff tangle with the law trying to explain why Len had disappeared.

Fortunately, he had no parents living, so inquiries from this direction were not forthcoming; but things might have gone badly for us had we not happened on a letter in his desk, in his own handwriting, explaining that he had gone away indefinitely to 'experiment.' Pretty vague, but since there was no disputing his handwriting after expert study, it put us in the clear again.

Both Greg and I lost something of our liking for pleasures as time went on. We hung around the apartment after our day's work, somehow half expecting Len would reappear. But nothing happened.

We bought astronomical journals and studied up the latest observations on Mars. Again we drew blanks—dry as dust articles, steeped in technicalities, carrying no clues at all. Inwardly, I think, we both bitterly reproached ourselves for the way we'd treated Len on the night of his departure. But after all—! Well, we're only human beings, and he had sounded pretty cock-eyed.

I once thought of writing up the whole truth, as I have done now—but at that time, I had no proof, and so refrained. It is only now, in the light of absolute facts, that I can put the real story together without fear. For at last, after four months of the most dreary winter I have ever known, a message arrived.

We had no idea then *how* it arrived. All we realized was that in an evening in early January, we returned from work to find a curious burnished cylinder lying on the sitting room table. The doors and windows of the apartment had been tightly locked, and our landlady was certain nobody had called, nor had she been up to our apartment all day.

It took us half an hour to get the cylinder unfastened, and out of it sprang a thick wad of heavy, parchment-like manuscript, covered with Len's familiar handwriting. I do not recall clearly what we did. My only recollection is that we pored over that manuscript together while seated on the divan—reading and reading until the fire went out and our eyes ached.

## LEN'S STORY

My very dear friends, Greg and Dick (the manuscript ran), I have reached Mars. Let me tell you of the strangeness, the infinite wonder, of my voyage.

I knew when I bade you 'Goodnight' that evening that I had also said 'Goodbye.' It was not long before I felt the fast governing compulsion of scientific forces overpowering me. I have a remembrance of rising from my bed, of a window moving swiftly towards me.

Then there was New York below me, spread out like a map, the rivers shining dull silver. It receded incredibly. I no longer saw a mighty metropolis, but all the continent of America. Then the whole western hemisphere of Earth, under its blanket of night.

Outward towards the eternal stars. I was cold, yes, but I only knew it with a certain sense of detachment. I seemed to have no body. I was either a disembodied thought hurtling over the wastes of space, else my body had been forced into complete subjection by my mind.

The latter theory I found later to be correct.

The stars, the sun, the moon...they were all around me, all save the sun vaguely terrifying in their solitary, inhumanly cold grandeur. For a while I saw and wondered at the titanic prominences of the sun, the unearthly glory of its corona. Then Mars was all that mattered to me in this vast, overpowering universe of powdered stars and cosmic dust—Mars, towards which I was hurtling almost with the speed of thought, faster than light itself. Onwards and onwards, silent and inevitable.

I reached Mars at last. It was night when I arrived. I do not clearly remember the last moments leading up to my arrival. I simply recall that I found myself alone in a waste of reddish desert, standing beside a long vanished riverbed. Yes, it was cold—horribly so. The air, too, was thin and poisonous. But somehow it did not seem to matter. My body was still adaptable as it had been in space.

And I had my body now because I could see it, but in the process of my journey I had lost my earthly attire. I was stark naked under the stars, a lone being in a graveyard of a world. Horrible, you think? No, not to me. I realized, I knew, that I was back on the world where once, very long ago, I had been born. My mind was completely in tune with my surroundings, so much in tune indeed that I experienced but little discomfort from the thin Martian air, cold, and light gravity.

Maybe you cannot conceive of an urge greater than life or death itself, an all-consuming force? That was what governed me. Food, sleep, rest—they meant nothing. I had to go on—to *her*! So I started off.

Perhaps I walked ten miles, fifty, a hundred—I do not know. But I do know that an unerring sense of direction was guiding me. I knew exactly what I expected to see, but when I reached the spot where I expected to see it, there was nothing. No, I am incorrect. There *was* something, like a ghost out of a past age.

Imagine it in the cold, constantly changing dim light of the two moons of Mars. Imagine those remains of a city—covered in a thick film of red dust, accumulated over countless centuries that rendered it invisible to Earthly telescopes—vast columns of naked stone reaching to the heavens, silhouetted against the stars—columns standing alone, the sentinels of a city that had once been great, all that remained of a titanic industry and purpose. A city, a world indeed, defeated by Nature, by lack of water, by crawling rust eating the very heart out of vast machines.

There it lay, the ruins of Ralidon, once master-city of Mars where I had been born. As I walked its sombre shadow-ridden recesses, brooded alone in the silence, it came back to me, little by little. I had lived here, yes—a Martian—and between Martians and Earthlings there is little physical distinction; The only difference is that Earthlings are grosser and less intelligent.

I saw her clearly now—tall, young, magnificently blonde, superbly commanding. Womanly indeed. My betrothed, Iana, my beloved.... Then what—? Yes! My experiments in the laboratory. Suddenly, the remembrance of a blinding explosion and darkness. So that was how I had died untold generations before? I had been blown to pieces by an experiment, torn away from my beloved, parts of my disintegrated being hurled in atomic bits into the cosmos.

Swirling, swirling, in the void. A bit here, a bit there. Parts of it on Earth, parts on Mars, parts not united. I lived again, in another body, reincarnated, but with no memory of my past.

Yes, I recollected that much as I sat there. The rest I had still to piece together in scientific explanation and order. For the moment, though, only one thing mattered.

Iana still waited, knowing far better than I had done at the time of the explosion, that I must one day come back. She was somewhere near in this buried ruin of a city. Had not her thoughts reached out to me across the gulf? Near—in suspended animation, her body locked but her mind free. Unguessable ages it must have searched for me, until now.

I got to my feet, moved with unerring purpose toward a fallen mass of masonry to the east of the city. Methodically I began to move aside the stones. I worked constantly, without fatigue, until the Martian dawn had come.

By that time, I had pulled aside endless numbers of stones, had raised the heavy slab covering the entrance to the underground mausoleum. On Earth I could not have shifted it. On Mars its weight was just sufficient for me.

Below there weighed an intense and heavy gloom, filled with the mouldering odour of age. There were sarcophagi all around me, some of them heavy stone of an early period, others transparent, glass-like metal containing still the embalmed bodies of Iana's own ancestors. They were embalmed, yes, but she—

At last I saw her, in a transparent coffin isolated from the others. Around its edges, where the glass fitted into sockets, were tiny wire-wound coils, glowing softly, still giving off energy that had so long held her in suspended animation.

I do not know how long I stood there contemplating her. She was so incomparably beautiful, so untouched by the ravages of time!—alabaster white, her masses of rippling golden hair flowing down over the whiteness of her pillow. Her hands were folded gently on her breast. She was smiling, ever so slightly.

For a long time, I hesitated over breaking that case, for to do it would mean her dissolution. I would be back again at that moment for which we had both waited so long. No, before I did that I must find a means of projecting to Earth the true story of my experiences. Only then could I feel that I had completely discharged my obligations to Earthly science for them to debate as they might see fit.

The mind of Iana directed me once again. In other quarters of the ruined city, underground, I found writing materials, together with a cylinder able to withstand the ravages of space and land on another world safely. But the complexity of the system of transit!

Four-dimensional it was—yes, four-dimensional and controlled by thought waves.

I spent hours pondering it, sitting m the matrix of complicated, unaged machinery determining all the mathematical factors for a reintegration of the cylinder on Earth—it was like a problem in television, how to reassemble the electronic image once it had been transmitted. Hours I spent, thinking, thinking, and thinking.... Until at last I was sure that I had mastered the problem sufficiently to project the cylinder not only to Earth, but with a certain mathematical certainty that would bring it right to my old apartment. Only you can know if I have been successful.

But for the interests of psychical and scientific research I must, I know, explain the scientific reason of my strange adventure.

You will know, or at least scientists will, that a given aggregate of molecules and atoms, whether in the form of a man or an inanimate object, can, by the law of chance, break up to reform one day in exactly the same pattern.

Sir Arthur Eddington has long ago propounded the chances of such a reformation, admitting that should the chance occur, it was something like one plus twenty-seven ciphers to one against it. Remember Sir Arthur's famous simile about monkeys plugging blindly on typewriters being able finally, by the law of chance, to type correctly all the books in the British Museum? Not through knowledge, but chance!

Some of us carry over from a past life the definite

memory of an existence gone before. We remember strange people and strange places. There are times when we are sure we have visited a certain place before in some other existence. Such a memory has always been with me—vague, subdued, blotted out by the urgency of events around me, at times—until recently, when I definitely felt telepathic impulses.

Time and again I must have died and lived once more, but by the inevitable law of chance, the atoms that had originally been the Martian began to move nearer and nearer to their original formation.

Each one had its own place in the composite that was me, but how many bodies I have had, in the interval, I do not know.

At last I was born as Len Brownson of Earth. There indeed was nearly the complete atomic formation I had once had. Daily in our life we lose atoms and pick up others. So it must have been with me. While I was still incomplete in atomic formation, I had only a vague knowledge of a vast might-have-been. But all around me, by mathematical law, those original atoms had drifted toward my one particular gravity. By degrees I picked them up in my daily life, unconsciously, until at last—on that evening when I so startled you—I realized that it was only a matter of hours before the original Martian form I had once would be in being again.

It happened. With what consequence? Surely it is clear? A specific buildup of atoms, no matter what the time period in which it occurs, relating to a particular organisation of atoms and surroundings, must fit itself to those conditions. Nothing I could do could prevent it. I would inevitably return by immutable law to those surroundings where those atoms had formerly been, because they were moulded to the pattern of that particular part of space.... Think for a moment of the thousands of people a year who mysteriously vanish. Why? Because they have achieved a condition they possessed ages ago, and have suddenly been transported into conditions appropriate to their changed state.

So I came back to Mars, conscious only of the former identity because I was he—am he—again. Only a vague memory of obligations to Earth remain. I know again of my beloved of that other life—Iana—know exactly what to do, because throughout the generations, she, the mistress of science and its laws, knew that one day I must return, as all things must return, and begin again. The universe itself is a cycle, so is the life within it.

But now I am through. You have the story, the explanation, to put on it what construction you will. When I open Iana's case, the artificial conditions in which she has lain so long will cease. In one sweep, time will catch up with itself. With her union with me, the existent atomic framework reformed from the past will shatter and pass away, assume their proper perspective in ageless time.

We shall vanish, only to be born again, together. Why? Because we are now both masters of mind and can control our birth—together, as it should have been so long ago.

The deserts of Mars will be truly empty. The eternal thin winds will sigh over them, carry memories of a former greatness; but for Iana and me, there will be a new beginning.

Goodbye, my very dear friends. I go now to fire the cylinder across the void to Earth. When that is done....

Iana!

# TWILIGHT PLANET

The great corridors of the master-city laboratories were deserted as Liana Fonray fled swiftly down them. She had slid past the none-too-watchful attendant in the entrance hall. She hurried with the easy grace of youth, a lightly-clad symphony in curves, her long yellow hair swept away from her lovely face by the breeze from the great ventilator shafts.

She had no right to be here at all. Not because she was a woman, but because she was not a scientist. The fact that she was the daughter of the Chief Physicist made no difference, for it did not make her one as well. If she were found, the law would not be lenient.

At a massive, bronze-coloured door she hesitated and glanced about her—still nobody in sight; the calm of the night was on the place. The staff had gone home except for one man—the one she sought with such recklessness.

For a moment she hesitated at the bronze door, then tried her gentle strength against it as she moved the catch. She was glad that it opened easily. It would not be necessary to disturb the room's inmate. Gracefully as a cat, she glided through the opening and closed the door behind her.

She stopped, her blue eyes wide in amazement at the immensity before her. She had never seen inside the main experimental hall of the physical laboratories before. Its mighty engines of science were somehow terrifying. The crisscrossing aisles and raised balconies made the place a gigantic, metallic spider's web.

For a moment the girl was confused. Then, at a distance, she caught sight of a solitary figure bending intently over a crackling electronic apparatus. Now and again great tubes filled with a myriad of colours—or, instead, a blaze of naked electrical light flared in blinding brilliance.

"Telsor!" the girl called. But the young man in the tunic and shorts was too preoccupied to notice her—or else he did not hear.

Liana went forward silently, keeping close to the machines so as not to make her appearance too sudden and disturb him. She watched the dark head bending over the equipment, the bronzed and muscular forearms working busily. Then a bewildering brilliance blazed forth with such intensity she clapped her hands to her eyes and screamed.

Her cry was sufficient to bring the young man to her side. As his arm went about her shoulders, she lowered her hands, and for a while the great space swam in a blazing sea of red and green. Then gradually her eyes adjusted themselves, and she saw Telsor Rolf's serious young face, his dark eyes concerned. Blue goggles were pushed up on his wide forehead.

"Liana, what are you doing here?" he demanded, with unmeaning roughness. "Do you realize you might have been blinded? Why did you come? You know it isn't allowed!"

"I just had to come," she answered simply. "A woman's place is beside the man she is going to marry, and I couldn't have you working here night after night, when working hours are over, without knowing what you are doing. Father has hinted at some great experiment. What is it?"

"I don't think you'd understand it," he answered, doubting. Then as he saw the look of disappointment on her face, he added with a smile, "I am trying to isolate an electron so that it can be viewed in a sub-atomic microscope."

"Oh! And would that be a—a useful thing to accomplish?"

"It would solve many problems of science, Liana. You see, by its very nature, the electron, as we understand it at present, cannot be viewed because the impact of light waves turned upon it are sufficient to deflect it. We know it is there, but science likes proof, something more than the mere probability that an electron exists in a given space."

From her expression the girl betrayed her lack of knowledge. But because Telsor had told it to her, and because Telsor was acknowledged to be a brilliant physicist despite his youth, she tried to evince interest. Going to the apparatus, she studied it.

"I'm trying first to isolate a carbon atom," Telsor

added, joining her. "The isolation of the electron itself will follow that. I've chosen carbon because it has certain exceptional qualities."

"Such as?" she asked curiously.

"Well, it is more than probable that life only exists at all because of the carbon atom. Life without carbon isn't even possible. Its atom consists of six electrons revolving around the nucleus.

"It differs from its nearest neighbours in the Periodic Table—boron and nitrogen—in that it has one electron more than the former and one fewer than the latter. That is why I am trying to isolate the solitary electron without, I hope, causing a total breakdown of the carbon atom itself."

The girl gave a little sigh and smiled faintly. Then, womanlike, she forgot all about the intricacies of science and strolled to the window. Even young Telsor Rolf was not so absorbed in his experiment that he could not appreciate how attractive she looked, standing there gazing out over the city. He joined her, put an arm about her shoulders.

The city was lighted brilliantly and the day-lamps had been extinguished. Normal daylight from a sun was unknown. The sun was a remote tennis ball blazing in a sky of stars and swirling planets.

The two young people did not look out on the universe from Earth, but from a world which had as its nearest neighbours a small planet with two racing moons, and a giant, cloud-girt world which poured its heat and ultra-violet radiations down upon them and so made up for everything the distant sun lacked—except light.

And this the scientists had overcome by devising energy lamps. For twelve hours they glowed in simulated daylight. Then, for another twelve, they were extinguished and recharged.

Telsor Rolf and Liana lived on a twilight planet, the only world they had ever known. Science, achievement, peace—all these things were present. But there still remained much to be discovered, how much they could not even guess unless the uncommon genius of Telsor Rolf could make an electron stand still.

"Funny," the young man murmured presently, his eyes on the starlit heavens, "to think that we are alone in the universe. We of this planet, I mean."

"Are we—alone?" The girl took the prodigious statement with amazing lightness.

"Alone on our little grain of sand," Telsor whispered. "We fight and struggle and die in the core of vast and meaningless distances, always aware that there are in those heavens as many worlds and suns as there are grains of sand on all the seashores of the world.

"And life alone came here—because of carbon, because of the blind play of inexplicable forces, because of the chemical reaction set up by naked cosmic rays pouring in from space. Sometimes—sometimes it's terrifying."

"Yes!" The girl's voice became awed and her blue eyes peered up into the incomprehensible mists of the Milky Way. "Yes, it is terrifying! And there is no life anywhere?"

"Not as far as our instruments can detect."

"Not even on that remote green star there, next to that reddish one?"

"Behind the reddish one," Telsor corrected, smiling. "It is much further away, third planet from the sun. No, there is no life even there. We are the fifth planet in order from the sun, and behind us stretch five more planets, four gas giants and one a pygmy.

"Yet we possess life. Probably, if it became necessary, we could exist equally well on the third or fourth planets from the sun. Our eyes could stand the glare of the much nearer sun. Evolution, artificial light, and the always present glow from the giant world nearest us have rendered that possible."

The girl turned from the window, reflecting.

"It is a wonderful thing—life," she mused.

"When I look at you, I am conscious of carbon atoms in their most enchanting link-up," Telsor laughed. Then he administered an almost boyish kiss and patted her rounded arm. "But you'll have to go, Liana. I must carry on my experiment. I dare not leave it now. In these tubes and apparatus elemental forces are at work, and if I stop them heaven knows what may happen."

"But—but surely I can stay and watch?" she pleaded.

He hesitated. "I'm afraid for you to. There might be an explosion. In trying to isolate an electron of carbon, I am using the atomic force of hydrogen for my energy. It's deadly unless rightly handled. A mistake might destroy this entire planet!"

"Then you would die, and I'd die with you," the girl murmured. "It is no more dangerous for you than for me. I'm staying! We can go home together later."

"Well—all right," Telsor agreed. Turning aside, he pulled up a heavy lead shield with a deep purple glass sunk in its centre. "Stand behind this," he ordered. "I'm taking no chances with so precious a spectator."

Liana obeyed eagerly and thereafter stood with her eyes glued to the glass and her slim body tensed in excitement as Telsor handled switches and buttons on his apparatus with the skill of a master.

She had not the remotest conception of his aims, even though she was a witness to his movements. Filigrees and spiders' webs of pure electrical energy writhed at times between polished balls. Earthing rods glowed under sudden huge electrical loads—and, now and again, that withering intensity of pure energy light gushed forth, turning the ceiling flood lamps to dirty yellow by comparison with its unholy glare.

Then, unexpectedly, came something different! There was a riot of electrical discharges, which clearly had no place in the experiment. Telsor began to work like a man possessed, obviously aware of some flaw in his experiment.

But he was not quick enough. There was an abrupt electric disturbance of immense power, which momentarily turned the apparatus pale green—then it went dead and smoky black, charred out of all shape. The glass in the tubes melted from inconceivable heat, the anode and cathode globes were useless as circular cinders on top of their corroded poles.

Telsor staggered backwards, wiping perspiration from his face. Liana crept from behind the shield and caught at his trembling arm.

"What—what happened?" she asked, wide-eyed.

"Too much power!" His voice was shaken. "I should have stepped down a bit—but I wanted maximum. I hammered the hydrogen atoms too much. They changed into helium. The sudden overload of energy due to the change in atomic makeup caused that sudden seize-up." He rubbed his naked forearms vigorously. "I got an unpleasantly large blast of cosmic rays from it, too!"

They were silent for a moment, rather terrified by the blind malignancy of natural forces. Then in a rather wondering voice, the girl asked a question.

"What's that there? A diamond?"

She bent down to pick up a glittering object from the shattered equipment, but Telsor dived and snatched her hand back. His lean, tense face was beside hers, peering down.

"It's—energy!" he whispered incredulously. "Atomic energy! Not the kind the scientists use for light and power, but the real thing. One atom breaks down and releases its energy, and immense sub-atomic disturbance produced thereby sets up ripples in the next nearest group of atoms. Then that too starts to break down. It's—progressive!"

They both straightened up slowly, searching each other's eyes.

"This is the thing scientists have dreaded for ages," Telsor said mechanically, his face suddenly old. "So far, chance has been kind. We've skirted the edge of unthinkable forces and tamed them, but a slip was always possible—and now I've made it!"

"But can't you extinguish it?" the girl asked, surprised. "It—it looks rather pretty, I think."

For a moment her ignorance of the tragic portent enraged Telsor, but with an effort he held himself in check.

"How can we extinguish the collapse of matter itself?" he demanded. "It'll grow—and grow—my God!" Stunned with the shock of foreseeing what might happen, he raced for the visiphone and switched to a number. In a moment the stern face of Liana's father merged onto the teleplate.

"Hello, Telsor!" he greeted, rather surprised. "Anything wrong?"

"I—I think so, sir," the young scientist stammered. "I want you to come to the main laboratory right away. I'm scared!"

He switched off and looked blankly at the girl.

"What do I do," she asked helplessly. "I can't let father find me here!"

"He'll have more things to worry about than your presence here, believe me," Telsor interrupted. He began to pace up and down anxiously as he waited for the expert to arrive. All the time he moved, he was conscious of a vicious little pricking in his skin, both on the exposed and unexposed parts. It was hardly attributable to electrical static. It was too sharp—like a thousand needles plunging deep.

Then at last there were quick footsteps in the corridor outside, and Elvan Fonray, the girl's father, came hurrying in. He was a tall, spare man with muscular legs and sinewy hands. High-cheekbones and taut lips revealed both thinker and man of action.

He glanced at his daughter, hesitated.

Then whatever he was going to say evaporated as he caught sight of the intense little spot of light amidst the wrecked equipment. He frowned at it. Snatching up a blue shield for his eyes, he went down on his knees and peered at the phenomenon closely. Real alarm was on his face when he stood up again.

"In the name of science, boy, what have you done?" he demanded, clutching Telsor's shoulder. "This is disintegrative atomic force! Matter cancer! It can bring the whole world down around our ears!"

Tremblingly, Telsor told of his experiment, and the lean-jawed physicist listened in concentrated attention.

"So you changed hydrogen into helium, did you? Hmm! That means that every four hydrogen atoms crushed together to form a helium atom would discharge a radiation of O-point-O-three, a surplus mass from the helium atom. Pure cosmic rays must have been generated for a brief instant, too, existing in the same form as in the free cosmos. Didn't you feel them?"

"I still do," Telsor muttered uneasily. "But I'm not unduly worried about myself. What do we do with—

*that*?"

"Obviously the violent interchange of energy started it," Fonray said, frowning perplexedly as he stared at it. "And I don't know how to stop it—but it has got to be stopped, if we work night and day until we accomplish it."

He broke off and swung to the attentive girl.

"What are you doing here, Liana?" he asked brusquely.

"I only came to see Telsor."

"Then you had no right! Go home immediately, and don't ever let me find you here again. Telsor will come and see you when he is free to do so."

Liana did not reply, but there was no resentment in her attitude. She knew that she had transgressed, and she knew too, that her father was unintentionally harsh in his anxiety. She gave Telsor a smile, then turned and went silently towards the door.

"This is serious!" Fonray declared, still frowning.

"It was a sheer accident, sir, and—"

"Yes, yes, of course it was an accident. All these damnable flukes of Nature are accidents—that is why we never have time to prepare a remedy. Bring me that neutralizer."

Telsor obeyed, and from then on he was only too glad to let his superior take charge of the situation. But his efforts with the neutralizer, a device for short-circuiting escaping energy into freer paths, were of no avail. The glowing spot became a larger glowing spot, consuming metal and stone as it expanded.

In half an hour of frantic effort, trying every scientific trick he knew, the physicist was no nearer a solution. The spot became a hole, radiating a light so intense that the two could no longer study it without shields before their eyes.

Fonray did not admit that he was beaten, even though inwardly he felt almost sure that he was.

"I'll have to consult the other scientists," he said finally, wiping his greasy face. "This is more than one man's brain can handle. You'd better go home. You look all in."

"I am," Telsor confessed. "I don't think that burst of cosmic rays did me any good since I had no protection suit on."

"In the pure, undiluted state they couldn't have. Off with you and get some rest!"

Telsor Rolf did not quite remember how he got home. He was in a peculiar state in which he was neither ill nor well. It was as if he was perfectly normal part of the time, then some inner disturbance would knock him off balance and he would become slightly delirious.

Certainly he had little consciousness of crossing the gulf of lighted city in an elevated monocar, even less of entering his apartment on the city's outskirts.

The thought of supper nauseated him. Instead, he poured himself a glass of essence, then sat thinking for a while, as the gentle exhilarating fluid surged into his bloodstream.

He began to feel better, less conscious of the accidental wrong he had done. That glowing hole devouring the heart of a fabulously costly physical laboratory no longer troubled him quite so much.

But it was only a brief reprieve from harassment, caused by the essence. In half an hour, as he prepared for bed, the effect had worn off and he was, if anything, more worried than ever.

It was as he stripped off his clothes and prepared to don his night attire that he stopped, staring at his legs and arms. They were covered with myriad little pimples, each with a dull red top, like tiny boils about to come to a head.

The sight of them stirred a deep inner feeling of uncleanness; the pain of them was manifested in those myriad needle pricks still grinding away so persistently at his body that he had become numbed to them.

When he looked in the full-length mirror, he saw that his face was in a similar condition. For several minutes he stood, wondering what he ought to do—then more from desperation than aught else he flung himself on the bed and drew the coverlet over him.

He closed his eyes—then opened them again abruptly. A sensation of the vilest headlong falling was upon him the moment he lowered his lids. It made him clutch the bed for support.

Again he tried, and again, forcing himself to have the courage to see where the fall would end. But it did not really end anywhere. It was as if he were falling endlessly through space itself, while past him, so prodigious was his speed, stars and suns streaked in ghostly, blazing splendour.

At last he groaned and sat up. Everything was normal the moment he opened his eyes. He switched on the light and stared blankly at the wall for a moment, rubbing his aching face. It was something in the quality of his hand as he rubbed that made him forget everything else. It was not the strong, yet withal spotted hand to which he was accustomed, but—

It was claw-like! Startled, he lowered it and stared.

The very bones of the hand itself had somehow retracted and the nails had shrunk to microscopic size. Even as he watched they vanished altogether under swift contraction of the skin. He did not actually feel the incredible metamorphosis. It was as of he were one mass of indescribable aches and pains, so that one more made little difference.

Dazed, he looked at his other hand, and found it had behaved the same way.

The shock was terrific. He scrambled from the bed and went again to the mirror, but so far nothing was wrong with the rest of his body—except for the spots, and these now were showing signs of disappearing. His face had indeed become normal—as far as the spots went—but either it was his imagination, or else his beard line was vanishing and giving his cheeks an almost girlish softness. It looked as though he had never had hair on his face at all!

Bemused, he stumbled back to the bed and sat on the edge of it, thinking, flogging his brain. That sense of earlier confusion was less noticeable now; it was more as if something were trying to gain access to his consciousness.

"Carbon," he whispered, and he did not know why he said the word. "Carbon! Carbon!"

Like a flash from a spark gap, his hazy conjectures leapt into clear realization. He jumped up and began to talk to the empty room.

"Carbon! I have carbon atoms. Everything has carbon atoms! Cosmic rays, in the beginning, caused life. Because of them constant mutations are occurring, especially in man. Life only exists in the universe at all because carbon has the power to comingle with other elements in endless variety.

"I was exposed to pure cosmic rays for a brief space. They affected the carbon atoms in my makeup. I am *evolving*! And evolving fast! Mutation upon mutation, even as the minutes pass by."

He paused, his face deathly white. He had spoken truth, and he knew it. He could feel the warmth of accelerated metabolism flowing through him. He had no thermometer handy, but he guessed his temperature to be well above normal already.

His readiness to believe in his own discovery started a new train of thought. First and foremost he was a scientist, and even if he himself were the victim of science's deadly power, he wanted to know the why and wherefore.

A little calmer, he sat down again and studied his hands, his mind rippling under new conceptions.

"I am evolving—that is established," he muttered. "In that case my brain must keep pace with it. The body cannot evolve without the brain doing likewise.

"If cosmic rays reacting on carbon atoms produced the fluke of life on this world, what produced intelligence? To knit together the chemical aggregates of life did not give them the power to think! Whence came that?"

But he was asking himself an impossible question. Though he could sense the gradual expansion of his conceptions as his brain underwent mutational changes, he was still not ready to solve this greatest of all scientific problems.

Far more settled in his emotions now that he knew he was tackling an incredible scientific fortuity, he turned and went back to bed. That sense of deadly falling was absent now, and he realized it had probably been caused by the changing action of the fluid of balance above his ears. But if the falling was absent, weird mental visions were not.

He could feel himself alive with conceptions—advanced ideas of what he had already learned, for even brain mutations could not tell him what he did not know. It was simply that his known knowledge was able to expand vastly, where formerly it had been limited.

He remembered the soft buzzer of the synchroclock announcing four in the morning—then he fell asleep.

The city day-lights were on as usual when he awoke, but with their radiance was mixed a pallid, steady glow that had no right to be there. For several minutes he lay trying to assimilate things—then he remembered.

He jerked up his head, then let it tall back again with a gasp of anguish at a wrenching pain in his neck. It was as though his head had become too heavy for him to raise it.

It was because his head had become too heavy! His thin, wizened hands went over its huge, bulging pate. His hair had gone. He could feel bony eyebrow ridges, the distension of veins on the taut skin of his skull. His vision, however, was undisturbed, in fact it was unnaturally clear.

His legs had shrunk even as his arms, his chest and hips too. Breathing was difficult. Gently he eased his hands under the back of his head and so, after some effort, got himself into a sitting position, supporting his egregious dome in his cupped hands, elbows on his knees.

The mirror caught his reflection as he turned towards it. For some reason he was not shocked. He had expected it. Science had said evolution must produce something like this—a wild travesty of a man, a baroque, with a brain-case so big his neck could not support it—a body so delicate it was fed by force of will alone.

He was still Telsor Rolf. He realized that. But gone were the thoughts of the previous night—of the desirability of marrying Liana Fonray, of youth together, of conquering the secrets of Nature. Such things no longer interested him. Still holding his head he got up and looked through the window. That light added to the day-globes was immediately explained.

From the centre of the city was emanating an irresistible blinding glare—the blaze of pure devouring energy, where matter was being consumed with a speed proportionate to the area of the disturbance. The heart of the city must have been eaten away during the night, and no doubt there was a mine in the ground of corresponding depth. End of the planet? Well, perhaps.

Telsor turned clumsily and staggered towards a chair. Then, supporting his head against the edge of the metal table he began to unscrew the chair legs from the seat and used them as a rough cage. This he fixed on his shoulders and under his chin and the back of his head. Now he had a support he could learn to walk all over again.

He was just getting along nicely when his apartment doorbell rang. He hesitated, then with considerable effort lurched across the room and gazed upon his visitor.

"Telsor, you've got to come—"

Liana stood on the threshold, her gush of words stopped. She fixed her eyes on the incredibly dwarfish figure with the mighty cranium—then her legs gave way and she sprawled on the carpet.

Telsor stood looking down at her, baffled. Then he shut the door and tried to lift her in his arms. She was far too heavy. All he could do was seize her under her armpits and drag her to the divan, against which he propped her head and shoulders.

After a few minutes she began to recover. Telsor stood watching her intently, saw again that look of incredible horror sweep over her face.

"I know," he whispered, his voice reedy and cracked. "I know what you are thinking, Liana. But I am Telsor Rolf, just the same. I have evolved. In fact I. am still evolving. I don't know where it is going to end."

"Evolved?" she repeated huskily. "But how?"

"Those cosmic rays—last night. They mutated me several centuries ahead. The last men on this planet will look as I do now."

Realization seemed to strike her. Her horror of the discovery was clearly outweighed by something else.

"There won't be any last men on the planet!" She scrambled to her feet as she spoke. "The planet's being eaten up! That atomic force is eating it away! We're evacuating everybody from the area."

"To where?" Telsor asked tonelessly. "Space travel is an art we have not yet mastered—and that is the only way out."

The girl stared at him fixedly, dumb horror in her blue eyes.

"I know," she said, in a dead voice. "It's just cheating death until it catches up, I suppose. But dad sent me to tell you that there might be a way if you'll come and help."

"There is no way, Liana, take it from me. I have gained knowledge centuries ahead of the present, and no power of man's devising can conquer devouring atomic force. But the space travel problem I can work out—and quickly.

"The best thing is for all of you to evacuate as planned. In the meantime I'll work out a means of travelling space. Now go! Please!"

Liana turned towards the door, looked back at him once more in horrified wonder—then she went.

Space travel—of course he could conquer it! The theories he had had as the normal Telsor Rolf were now expanded with his brain's mutations into absolute knowledge. He went to the table and pulled a sheet of foil from the drawer, held the stylo-pen in his unaccustomed claw.

Carbon? Intelligence? Carbon? Intelligence?

The two problems and the missing link between danced in his brain as he forced himself to think on the profoundest riddles of science. What gave intelligence to carbon atoms to make them thinking beings?

He nearly had it—then the answer slipped by him again and he began to wrestle with the complexity of space travel. But even as he made the first awkward notations with his clumsy hand, he realized that the end of his evolution was not yet. Further anguishing changes swept through him and there came a weird foreshortening of vision. With it a swift alteration of his limbs.

He was shrinking at an incredible speed—shrinking like a rubber man with the air escaping from him. The stylo became too ponderous for his minimizing hand. His head slipped inside the rough cage. The table seemed to swell and grow away from him.

He did not lose consciousness during his descent into remote smallness. Rather, his brain seemed to be sharpened. How long it lasted he did not know, but he did realize that when the evolution was finished, he was not seeing with his eyes or hearing with his ears.

Both states were mental, and what body he possessed was a long bar-like creation floating gently in the breeze of the apartment.

The apartment itself seemed nearly as big as a planet, and the open window was the sky.

Bacteria! He realized it suddenly. The evolution beyond evolution. Scientists had averred that life would finally pass into the form of indestructible bacteria, the toughest form of life in creation—able to resist the boiling of water and the frigid cold of space. Man must become bacteria—finally.

He had become that—intelligent beyond anything he had ever known, but was it finality? He suspected other things were to happen even yet before the mutations of atomic structure came to an end.

Dimly he was aware of the disaster of the happening. He knew how to conquer space, yet he had not the physical means of passing on his information.

As he drifted through the window, entirely invisible, and floated amidst the rocks of dust in the atmosphere, he saw below him the planet he was powerless to save. It was vast to his mental eyes—incredibly vast—seared in the centre by a gaping, blinding hole of intense white.

From it he could see people milling in ever thickening crowds, spreading away from the scene of the disturbance like the tentacles of an octopus. Flight, to stave off the evil hour—flight, while they waited for him to solve the problem!

He would have felt sorrow, but emotion was dead.

It was some time before he realized his will power was such that he had no need to rely on the drifting of the wind to guide his course. So he hovered and watched and the awful flame of energy was powerless to blind him. The thunder of collapsing rock was unable to deafen him. He had gained a brief but magnificent immunity to the forces ot Nature gone mad.

Perhaps it was hours—weeks—years. He could not be sure. His sense of time had gone. But he saw the whole panorama below him drag to its awful end. There came a time at last when the consuming fire had spread so far from the centre that the people were round the edge of the dying planet in a black and jagged fringe.

He pictured them cowering before the glare, seared by the awful heat. He pictured Liana, her sightless eyes staring helplessly into the gulf, her lovely form lashed by the first awful flames of the devouring fire. She would be wondering why he had not kept his word.

Then came the incredible vision of a world collapsing, of the whole planet exploding into whirling fragments of blazing rock, shooting outwards as myriads of separately burning fragments, doomed to consume themselves and leave, perhaps, tiny burned-out husks in which atoms would form again; Meteorites, maybe— even a band of asteroids. For some of the trapped people, there had been the more merciful death of space cold.

The planets moved and swung majestically under the gravitational changes as their tortured brother died.

Then it was all over—but not for Telsor Rolf.

Again the mutational surge was passing through him. He realized it even as the swinging of gravity fields forced him through the black void against his will. And the void held energies and cosmic rays in their pure form.

They were ripping at him, battering apart his bacterial make-up. He was moving with terrific speed, down at last towards a green world, slowly swinging to a standstill as the changes subsided.

He went through cloud, down and down into a world of steam and dank warmth. Then came sudden agony through his body as though it were being split into a million fragments, as though he were in a million places at the same time.

He seemed to be in the dark now, moving majestically round a sun. There were six of him moving round the sun. There were six suns! Twice times six—a million of him revolving round a million suns—two million—three....

He had split into electrons, was going round the nucleus.

There were six—carbon! And the truth came to him. Life had come to his world because just such an accident as this had happened there too. Why not, if Time were a circle?

A thinking being had been split into carbon atoms, and each atom had retained the power of thought! With the processes of life, the thought-power—the life energy as some scientist had called it—would be handed down to the otherwise lifeless molecular build-up.

Carbon had the power of thought!

And life would come here—to this world man would call Earth. Man would wonder how life had arrived, even more so what made it think. They would count four planets and then gaze at a belt of asteroids and wonder how it came to be there.

As Telsor Rolf had done, they too would wonder.

But for Telsor Rolf wonder was no more. *He knew.*

# ABOUT THE AUTHOR

British writer JOHN RUSSELL FEARN was born near Manchester, England, in 1908. As a child he devoured the science fiction of Wells and Verne, and was a voracious reader of the Boys' Story Papers. He was also fascinated by the cinema, and first broke into print in 1931 with a series of articles in *Film Weekly*.

He then quickly sold his first novel, *The Intelligence Gigantic*, to the American magazine, *Amazing Stories*. Over the next fifteen years, writing under several pseudonyms, Fearn became one of the most prolific contributors to all of the leading US science fiction pulps, including such legendary publications as *Astounding Stories*, *Startling Stories*, *Thrilling Wonder Stories*, and *Weird Tales*.

During the late 1940s he diversified into writing novels for the UK market, and also created his famous superwoman character, The Golden Amazon, for the prestigious Canadian magazine, the Toronto *Star Weekly*. In the early 1950s in the UK, his fifty-two novels as "Vargo Statten" were bestsellers, most notably his novelization of the film, *Creature from the Black Lagoon*.

Apart from science fiction, he had equal success with westerns, romances, and detective fiction, writing an amazing total of 180 novels—most of them in a period of just ten years—before his early death in 1960. His work has been translated into nine languages, and continues to be reprinted and read worldwide.